"You've got freckles," Ernie said.

Hannah frowned. His proximity and his clean male scent were calling up that dark, warm feeling again. Lord, what a nice face he had. Nice face, nice thighs . . .

"Yes, I know," she said dryly. "What are you doing here? I thought you were going to South Dakota."

"So did I. I got to thinking about the kid—"

"We're doing all right," she interrupted.

"—and you," he finished.

And me? she almost said, the dark, warm feeling spreading, making her knees weak, making her heart pound. "You didn't have to come back," she said with as much conviction as she could muster.

"Yeah, that's what I told myself the whole time I was getting my knee patched up, and all the way down I-35—in both directions. Someho~~w, I ~~ ~~self be~~lieve it . . ."

Cinda Richards

Hailing from North Carolina, Cinda Richards confesses she has had three great secrets in her life. "I was in love with Roy Rogers, I wanted to learn to play the piano, and I wanted not only to write but to be read. I didn't do anything about the last two secrets until I hit my thirties, playing 'The Little Drummer Boy' in my first piano recital when I was thirty-three, and publishing my first short story on a small scale when I was thirty-four. Roy Rogers is still on hold, since my husband of twenty years might not understand—even if he did once give me a Roy Rogers alarm clock."

Cinda writes almost constantly now, and when she's not brewing a new novel, she works as a public health nurse. Literary acquaintances and medical friends alike find her combination of careers odd. Fellow health-care workers often exclaim, "Can you believe that sweet nurse writes romances?" Well, not only does she write them, but she claims to have a wonderful time doing it.

In between all that activity, she also mothers a teenage son, who recently pronounced (not without a certain amount of pride), "I've got the weirdest mother in the whole class!" As Cinda Richards says, "What more could a woman want?"

Dear Reader:

A tall, dark, handsome, and ornery cowboy and a fair-haired, debonair English lord are our November heroes, portrayed by Cinda Richards and Christina Dair, respectively. Cinda's last Second Chance at Love novel, *Fire Under Heaven* (#382), was spotlighted in *Rave Reviews* magazine, and drew some of the most enthusiastic fan letters we've ever received. Christina's previous romance, *Tempting Patience* (#319), was awarded four stars by reviewer Melinda Helfer, who predicted "quite a future in the genre" for Christina (*Romantic Times*, #26).

One From the Heart (#426) by Cinda Richards should have special appeal for westerners and fans of western romances, for the protagonists are a rodeo Romeo and a rancher's daughter. Ernie Watson, a half-Cherokee cowboy who was a secondary character in *Such Rough Splendor* (#280), falls instantly in love with Hannah Browne when their eyes meet over Hannah's sleeping niece, Petey. Seems Hannah's beautiful, unpredictable sister, Libby, has run off, leaving Ernie with instructions to deliver Petey to Hannah. Hannah fears that Ernie's still carrying the torch for Libby, but he's determined to convince Hannah *she's* the Browne sister he loves. *One From the Heart* is an entertaining and poignant mixture of intense emotion and steamy romantic tension that's guaranteed to touch *your* heart.

In *Nights in Shining Splendor* (#427) by Christina Dair, madcap American heiress Iris McCormick utterly captivates Nigel, Lord Burke, a British baron who eventually pursues free-spirited Iris all over England and Wales. Though she loves Nigel, Iris feels she's too hopelessly Bohemian to fit into his aristocratic lifestyle—until he shows her the streak of devil-may-care wildness that lies beneath his proper, lordly demeanor. The zany escapades here bring to mind the smash-hit film *Arthur,* and those of you who are partial to English estates and titled nobility will definitely find *Nights in Shining Splendor* your cup of tea!

Along with the sparkling entertainment in this month's Second Chance at Love romances, Berkley brings you a rich panoply of additional romantic reading. *Dansville* by Robin McCorquodale is a grand, smoldering contemporary Texas romance about a woman who refuses to compromise and the younger man brought to maturity by her love; *Looking Glass Years* is bestselling author Jill Gregory's first historical epic, the story of a 19th-century woman of substance determined to realize her dreams and marry the man she loves more than life itself; and *Forever the Flame*, Norah Hess's latest historical romance, is set on the lawless Kentucky frontier. Medical-romance enthusiasts won't want to miss *Half Life* by Priscilla Scherer, R.N., in which a nurse finds herself torn between professionalism and her love for an eminent doctor, while Regency fans will be pleased that we're reissuing *The Grand Sophy* by Georgette Heyer and *A Marriage of Inconvenience* by Elizabeth Mansfield. Our new Barbara Cartland Camfield novel is *The Love Puzzle,* and we're reissuing a romantic novel by Agatha Christie writing as Mary Westmacott, *Absent in the Spring.* You may also enjoy reading *Dancing on my Grave*, the riveting autobiography of prima ballerina Gelsey Kirkland, telling of her triumphant recovery from drug addiction and discovery of redemptive love with her husband and co-author Greg Lawrence.

We continue to enjoy reading your letters, so please keep writing to share your thoughts and opinions on Second Chance at Love. We appreciate your enthusiastic support of our books, and we want to go right on being responsive to your desires and preferences. Since many readers inquire whether they can order Second Chance at Love romances by mail, we'd like to call your attention to the mail-order coupon at the back of every Second Chance at Love book.

Until next month, happy reading!

With best wishes—

Joan Marlow

Joan Marlow, Editor
SECOND CHANCE AT LOVE
The Berkley Publishing Group
200 Madison Avenue
New York, NY 10016

SECOND CHANCE AT LOVE™

CINDA RICHARDS
ONE FROM THE HEART

B
BERKLEY BOOKS, NEW YORK

CHAPTER ONE

THE FIRST TIME Hannah Rose Browne saw John Ernest Watson, she had two thoughts. The first was a passage from the Song of Solomon: "Turn away thine eyes from me, for they have overcome me"; the second was the certain knowledge that the compelling sadness she saw in this man's eyes had something to do with her sister Elizabeth—no great piece of detective work on her part, because he was standing on her doorstep with Elizabeth's sleeping child slung over his shoulder.

"Are you going to let us in or not?" he asked, turning around so she could see Petey's face. He sounded tired and more than a little harassed.

"What are you doing with Elizabeth's daughter?"

Hannah demanded as he stepped inside. He paid her no attention whatsoever.

"Where's the bedroom?" he asked, limping in the wrong direction. He was a tall man with dark eyes and a dark mustache. He needed a shave, and he was wearing faded jeans with a red plaid shirt and a denim jacket. His oversize black cowboy hat made him look as if he'd just dropped in from a smokeless tobacco ad or a dusty cattle drive of the last century.

"That's the kitchen," she said when he reached the kitchen door.

"Well, thanks a lot, lady. I've been driving for seven hours, I'm hungry, I got *no* sleep, I got a knee that needs sewing up, and somehow I got to get to Rapid City, South Dakota, by tomorrow afternoon. So go ahead—let me wander all over the dang place—it's not like I'm in a hurry."

"You didn't answer me," Hannah said, unimpressed by his troubles. "What are you doing with Petey?"

"I'm trying to give her to you if you'll tell me where I can put her down!" he said loudly enough to cause the little girl over his shoulder to lift her head for a moment. "Go back to sleep now, Pete," he whispered to her, rocking her back and forth. He glanced at Hannah and then back again, as if her physical appearance had only just registered. His eyes swept over her, face to breasts to hips and back to her breasts again before he finally met her eyes. Hannah stared at him calmly—hoping she looked much calmer than she felt. She had experienced —and enjoyed—many a lingering male appraisal in her time, but he was quite bold in assessing whatever he thought she might be hiding under the baggy sweat suit she was wearing, bold enough make her pulse quicken and her cheeks flush. The dark eyes that now probed hers offered no apology. If anything, he seemed more annoyed—as if he'd found her more physically attractive than he'd expected, sweat suit or not, and that was the last thing in the world he needed.

"In here," Hannah said after a moment, trying to ignore her response to whatever it was he thought he was doing. It wasn't that her response was unpleasant so much as it was a surprise. She had always found the archaic keep-'em-barefoot-and-pregnant attitude men in this part of the country seemed to have unappealing, yet she couldn't deny that in this case she *had* responded. In that one long look, he had suddenly changed from a generic cowboy to one who was most definitely individual—and male. She led the way to the bedroom, now intensely aware of that maleness. Clearly, Elizabeth wasn't with them, and Hannah was going to have to take care of first things first. She had been working on several scripts for a furniture-outlet commercial, and she had to move a stack of papers and a bean-bag lap desk before he could put her niece down on the bed. He did so gently—after figuring out he had to first stand still so that Hannah, flustered now by his proximity, could get out of his way.

"Ernie?" Petey murmured sleepily as the two of them tucked Hannah's patchwork quilt carefully around her.

"Yeah, Pete, what is it?" he said kindly.

And suddenly Hannah realized who John Ernest Watson was: Elizabeth's childhood friend, Ernie, the famous bull-dodging clown on the professional rodeo circuit, or perhaps infamous was a better word. He was supposed to have become a hard-drinking womanizer in recent years—if she could believe Elizabeth. She felt a familiar pang of annoyance. Whatever else Elizabeth was, she was truthful—when it suited her. And God only knew what he was doing with Petey or what Elizabeth was up to now.

"You're the rodeo clown," Hannah said, feeling a little better about the situation and wondering why. She carefully avoided looking at him, because she could feel him looking at *her*. Again.

"Yeah, well, that's the way I like to think of myself. *The* Rodeo Clown."

"Ernie," Petey murmured again, "don't make it dark."

"I won't, baby. Go to sleep—she's afraid of the dark," he said to Hannah.

"I lost Cowpoke," Petey said sleepily, feeling around under the quilt.

"Aw, we left him in the car," Ernie said. "I'll get him—unless Miss Hannah will do that for us so old Ernie doesn't have to walk with his bad knee and everything."

Hannah glanced at him. He gave her a warm, persuasive grin; she gave him an arch look, promptly losing the feeling of reassurance she'd just had. Any man who would use a child to manipulate a situation to his advantage was capable of anything, bad knee or not.

"Yes, please, Aunt Hannah," her niece said politely.

"Petey, where's your m—"

"Say hello to Aunt Hannah, Pete," Ernie interrupted, giving Hannah a sharp dig in the ribs with his elbow.

"Hello, Aunt Hannah," Petey said dutifully, briefly opening her eyes. "Are you surprised? Ernie said you'd be surprised."

"Boy, am I ever," Hannah said in all truthfulness. She wanted to bend down and kiss her niece on the forehead, but somehow, with Ernie Watson watching, she wasn't quite at ease enough to do it. Petey was a sweet child, though not beautiful as children went, having a sort of Holly Hobby look, with her light brown braids and freckles. In fact, she looked more like her Aunt Hannah than her exquisitely blond and blue-eyed mother.

"So," Hannah whispered to her. "What's a—Cowpoke?"

"Brown," Petey whispered back.

"I see," Hannah teased. "I go out into the parking lot—and I keep looking until I find *brown*." She punctuated the "brown" with an awkward little pat, glancing at Ernie and forcing herself not to ask questions about Elizabeth now.

"I'll go get him," he said. "I can do it faster than I can tell you what he is. Kiss," he said to Petey, tapping the spot on his cheek where he wanted it. Petey obliged him while he shot a quelling look at Hannah. Whatever was going on, he didn't want her to interrogate Petey about it. He limped away, coming back in a few minutes with an obviously homemade stuffed bear. It was indeed brown, and it was dressed in a sequined western suit with fringe that made it look like a poor man's mascot for Porter Wagoner.

"Cowpoke," he explained, holding up the bear as he came into the bedroom. "And don't ask me why." Petey had already gone back to sleep, and he quietly tucked the bear in beside her.

"Mr. Watson . . ." Hannah said as soon as they had moved into the hall.

"Ernie," he corrected her, and he seemed to be looking for something.

She ignored his invitation to familiarity. He'd gotten more than familiar enough for her liking. "Mr. Watson," she repeated, but he held up his hand to stop her.

"Where is Elizabeth?" she asked anyway, whispering so she wouldn't wake up Petey.

"I don't know," he whispered back, leaning close to her so that she got the barest whiff of his definitely appealing masculine scent. "My knee's bleeding again, Hannah. I need your bathroom," he added in a normal tone of voice.

She looked down at his knees. One jeans leg had a big red stain, which was widening in an alarming manner.

"Oh, Lord—in there, in there," she said, trying to wave him in the right direction, all the while trying to assess how it was she came to have an unauthorized child in her bed and a bleeding cowboy wandering all over the place. She didn't mean to go along with him into the bathroom, but he was holding on to her by that time, his big hand warm and firm on her shoulder, and somehow she just *went*.

"Help me get my pants off," he said, standing on one foot while he took off his jacket. Hannah looked at him, her pulse rate kicking up again.

"Hey," he said, grinning and chucking her under the chin. "I generally have to know a woman awhile before I drop my pants, but this is an emergency."

"You need a doctor!" Hannah insisted, frowning because the idea of having to get him out of his tight-fitting jeans was costing her what little composure she had left—and he knew it. He handed her his hat.

"No, honey, I need to get my pants off. Can you help me with that boot?"

She didn't budge.

"What's the matter?" he asked innocently.

"Nothing," she said in a tone of voice that positively reeked of untruth.

"What is it you think I'm going to do, Hannah?" He was smiling and trying to look into her eyes.

"Nothing!" she said again, making herself look at him.

"Well, I'm going to bleed to death if you don't help me."

"Lord!" she said, abruptly kneeling down and tugging at the boot while still holding his hat. He let out a yelp of pain, and she turned his foot and the hat loose, nearly causing him to fall.

"Wait—wait!" he said, hopping until he could put the lid down on the commode and sit. "Now pull."

"How did you get in this fix anyway?" she felt compelled to ask, largely because it kept her mind off the fact that she was having to put her hands all over him.

"Same way I always do. A high-kicking bull—"

She got his boot off, then his pants, trying not to look at his noticeably manly thighs. A random comparison image—*soccer-player thighs*—flitted through her mind, and she glanced up at him in spite of her attempts to stay as removed as possible from the situation. He was grinning from ear to ear.

She frowned again and backed out of the bathroom, leaving him alone with a stack of towels and cold water running in the sink, stumbling over a boot on the way out. After a moment she came back in to offer him antiseptic. And to prove to herself he was having no effect on her. He shooed her away, a bit irritably, she thought, informing her that anybody—even she—should know soap and water was the best thing to clean out a cut.

"No, I didn't know," she muttered to herself when she was back in the hall. Somehow she was holding his darn hat again. She hovered around for a minute, mentally chastising herself because his muscular thighs and overt assessment had rattled her so. He was one of those flirtatious, good-ole-cowboy types, and she should have more sense than to respond to his heavy-handed technique. She'd never responded to that type before, she assured herself, and she certainly wasn't going to start now. She went to check on Petey. Her niece was sleeping quietly with her flashy cowboy bear clutched close. She reached out to turn off the light, then remembered that Petey was afraid of the dark.

Petey, Petey, she thought. She closed her eyes for a moment. Where the devil was Elizabeth, and what was she supposed to do with a four-year-old child? She had to go to work tomorrow; she had no place to leave Petey, and she couldn't take her along. She had no vacation days left for the year—

"Hannah?" Ernie Watson called from the bathroom.

"What!" she said, giving in to the exasperation she was feeling. "Lord!" she said under her breath. God only knew what she was supposed to do about him, either—particularly if he was going to look at her the way he did and insist on having his pants off.

He wanted her to search through his jeans pockets for some butterfly adhesive bandages. Then he gave her the choice of either taping the cut closed with the butterflies while he held the gaping edges together or vice versa. She chose the latter—because he did need help—but she was able to accomplish it only by closing her eyes. First aid was definitely not her forte, and touching this man's bare knee wasn't helping.

"So. Hannah," he said after a moment. "What's new?"

She opened her eyes. "What's new?" she repeated, momentarily bewildered by the triteness of the question . . . given the recent turn of events. She found herself staring into his dark eyes again. Something about them reminded her of the grave dignity of old daguerreotype photographs, and the sadness she'd noted earlier was not diminished by the teasing grin he was still wearing. "Oh," she said airily, "not much. Why?"

His grin broadened, then faded away. "You know your sister's a long-term nut case, don't you?" The words were light, but, oh, those sad eyes. He pulled several sterile gauze pads out of his shirt pocket and gave them to her to open. She tore open the ends of the packs and carefully took the gauze squares out while he kept pressure on the cut.

"Yes, well...I didn't know Elizabeth until I was sixteen," she said, trying to be careful where she looked, a difficult task when one had only arresting eyes, naked muscular thighs, and a bleeding cut to choose from. "I can only vouch for the last nineteen years or so."

She and Elizabeth had been separated by their parents' divorce when Elizabeth was four and she was two. Hannah had gone to live with their mother, while Elizabeth had remained with their father in the bosom of one of the most successful ranching families around Tulsa. But it was Hannah who had been the better off, growing up poor but happy, bouncing from motor court to trailer park in the vagabond life their free-spirited mother had chosen.

Shamelessly spoiled, her sister Elizabeth had had every material thing money could buy. She had been born with their mother's beauty and strong will and their father's reckless charm. Everyone loved Elizabeth, especially Hannah—and probably John Ernest Watson. There was something in her that inspired mindless devotion. But to expect anything in return for it was like waiting on the corner for a streetcar—in Death Valley.

"Shouldn't you put something on that first?" Hannah asked worriedly as he arranged the gauze over the cut. It looked awful, and soap and water hardly seemed enough. She raised her eyes and found him staring at her. This look was neither grave nor teasing. It was a man-woman look, one that quickened her already hustling pulse, one that made her forget what she was talking about, and one that was definitely not suitable for the person he knew only as "Elizabeth's sister." Once again she had the feeling that while he might find her attractive, he also considered her something on the order of a fate worse than death. Then he smiled abruptly, and she couldn't tell if she'd imagined it or not.

"Hannah, will you let me handle this? A man who's been kicked and hooked by a damn cow as many times as I have knows what to do. Reach into my jacket pocket, will you? There's an elastic bandage in there. So why did your mother keep you and Elizabeth apart?" he asked, all business now and obviously interested in the subject she'd had no more sense than to introduce. She found the bandage and handed it to him. She also found herself answering him.

"She didn't keep us apart. It was my father—part of the divorce agreement, I think. Elizabeth was eighteen when she decided she ought to get to know us. I imagine the Tulsa part of the family had a fit. Anyway, there she was at the door one day—rich, gorgeous. I expected to hate her guts, but I didn't. She was sort of like a little lost child or something, you know?" She glanced at him. Yes, she thought immediately. He knew.

"I don't understand why Elizabeth would leave Petey with you," she said, getting back to one of the two problems at hand. Her other problem was that he didn't need her help anymore, and she should gave gotten herself out of the bathroom, but she could hardly move without touching him.

"Elizabeth trusts me," he said simply, not looking up from his bandaging. "I spent a big part of my life looking after your sister. You can probably guess what that was like," he added with a candor she hadn't expected. "She came to see me at the rodeo in Oklahoma City— hell, I hadn't seen her since before she took up with that last poor fool she married. How many husbands does that make now, anyway?"

"Three," Hannah said dryly. "That we know about."

He almost smiled, and he still wasn't looking at her. She could almost feel the effort he was putting into that —*not* looking at her. Which was crazy, since they'd only just met.

"So the next thing I know, Elizabeth's gone again and I find Petey asleep in my car with a note in her pocket that says I'm to bring her here to Dallas to you. I had a hell of a time finding you. You're not in the phone book, and you didn't work anymore where Elizabeth said you were working . . . and I could tell right off how you were really expecting us." He glanced up to find her studying him thoughtfully.

"What?" he asked, and this time his eyes frankly met hers. She was, quite honestly, making an appraisal of her own, trying to decide what it was about this man that unnerved her so. He wasn't *that* handsome. True, he had beautiful dark eyes—and a bit of the lost-waif look that Elizabeth had. He smelled of soap and leather and the out-of-doors. His hair was thick and very black, clean and shiny and in bad need of a trim. She couldn't decide whether he ought to get rid of the mustache and the five-o'clock shadow or not. It was certainly . . . intimate looking.

"I . . . was just trying to remember what I know about you," she said, being less than candid herself. It was odd, she thought, that he should affect her the way he did and yet be so easy to talk to. But that was probably because he behaved as if his long-standing friendship with Elizabeth somehow extended to her. He obviously felt he could be as cranky or inquisitive as he liked. Of course, there weren't many men one could just meet and still feel at ease with while they were bleeding and wearing nothing but underwear and a long-tailed shirt, whether they knew one's sister or not.

He gave a crooked smile. "I don't guess there's much for you to remember. My dad was a cowhand on the Browne ranch, and my aunt Mim was Libby's nursemaid from the time you and your mother left. It drove old man Browne—your dad—crazy that I associated with his precious daughter. See, my mother was Cherokee—and Mim, too. And if that wasn't enough, I was just the hired help. No, hell, I wasn't even that. I was just one of the hired help's relatives; I never tried to pass inspection and get hired. By the time you got to know Libby, my mama was dead and my dad had moved us off to New Mexico."

"My sister told me about you."

"Did she?" he asked, and Hannah had the distinct impression that while that thought pleased him, it also caused him pain.

"She told me what you just said. And that you're the only person in the world who calls her Libby. And you taught her to ride and to swim. And she didn't know what it was you thought was so great about New Mexico."

"I was glad to be in New Mexico by that time. It kept me from—" He didn't go on, glancing briefly into Hannah's eyes and then away. "So what else did she tell you?"

She hesitated. "Nothing," she decided. She wasn't going to tell him about the hard drinking and the womanizing.

"She tell you I was a drunk?" he asked point blank.

"Not—exactly."

"What, exactly?" he asked, glancing briefly into her eyes again. Hannah had the sudden feeling that this man could spot a lie in a second.

"She mentioned that you...had problems, and maybe you drank more than you should," Hannah said, trying to be tactful.

He gave a short laugh. "I'll just bet she did. Did she happen to mention that she was one of the problems? Did she tell you a few years ago I was damn fool enough to think she'd marry me? Man, I was dumb. Maybe she told you what a stupid bastard I was—"

"No, she didn't tell me anything about that," Hannah said too quickly. For some reason she couldn't fathom, she didn't want to be privy to Ernie Watson's pain, particularly if Elizabeth had caused it. "I'm...sorry it didn't work out," she added, feeling that somebody ought to be, because Elizabeth probably wasn't.

"Yeah," Ernie said, putting the finishing touches on his bandaging. "You're sorry, I'm sorry, but that didn't keep Libby from saddling me with child care for a week—whether I'm supposed to be a drunk or not. And I don't know what the hell I'm telling you all this for. Hand me my pants."

"You've had Petey for a week?"

"Yeah. My pants?"

"You took your own good time about getting in touch with me."

"I had problems of my own."

"You had problems? My sister is missing!"

"She's not missing—she's abandoned her kid. There's a big difference. I make my living on the rodeo circuit, Hannah. I don't do it for fun. I need the money. I couldn't take the time to bring Petey to you until now. And the note didn't mention whether you'd know anything about it."

She stood staring at him for a moment, then picked up his pants. But she didn't give them to him. She walked out of the bathroom with them instead.

"Hannah!" he called after her. "If you'll give me my pants, I'll get out of here."

"What?" she said absently, her mind in a turmoil as the complexities of the situation began to sink in. Her sister had been gone for a week, and Petey was going to be staying here with her—although she lived in an apartment complex that didn't allow children, had no extra money for sitters or day care, couldn't possibly take any days off without jeopardizing her job, and had an enjoyable no-strings relationship with Rick Archer, who was clearly pleased that she was as free to come and go as he was. "Don't you have any idea where Elizabeth is?" she asked as Ernie hobbled out of the bathroom carrying his boots. "She must have said something."

"I don't know where she went. I was hoping you would."

Hannah stared at him. He was serious.

"I haven't seen her for months," she said. She hadn't seen Petey for nearly a year.

He looked down at the floor and took a long breath. "Well, that's Libby. Hey," he said, looking up at her, "Don't worry. You know how she is."

"Don't worry?" she said incredulously.

"Look, I figure it's like this. You can let Libby drive you nuts or you can accept her the way she is."

"Oh, sure. That's easy for you to say. You're leaving, and this has got nothing to do with you. Or has it?" she asked suspiciously. There had to be some reason why a man would put himself out like this.

He took his jeans out of her hands and struggled until he got them on. "If you mean is Petey my kid, the answer is no. If she was, you wouldn't get her." He zipped up his jeans.

"And just what is that supposed to mean!"

"You figure it out. And I'm not getting tangled up with any more Browne women if I can help it, whether they're four years old or what."

Hannah's temper flared even though she did understand his attitude. And who asked him to get "tangled up" anyway? She and Petey weren't to blame for this. It was Elizabeth who had put him through an emotional wringer. If one associated with Elizabeth Browne, one had to expect that kind of thing.

"Where are you going?" she demanded. He had tugged his boots on and was hobbling into the kitchen.

"I just had this horrible thought," he said, flinging open the refrigerator door. "I knew it!" he said peering inside at a few containers of yogurt and diet soda. "You're one of those career women, right? You never eat and never buy any damn groceries, and you don't know the first thing about looking after a kid, do you?"

"I'll manage! Now, if you'll kindly get out of my

refrigerator and tell me how much I owe you, I'll pay you for your trouble." She picked her purse up off the kitchen counter and got out her checkbook, praying that the amount would be small.

"Lady, there's not enough money in the *world* to pay me for the trouble I've had." He slammed the refrigerator door shut. "Do you know how to take care of a kid, or don't you?"

"I told you I'd manage!"

"Yeah, well, that's not good enough. That kid— young as she is—has been through hell. You want to know how scared she is? She's so scared she hasn't asked once—not *once*—where her mother is. It's like she's afraid to know. Now, I brought her to you because Libby wanted me to, but damned if I'm leaving her with somebody who don't even eat right."

"Mr. Watson—" Hannah began, giving reason and civility a halfhearted try.

"Ernie!" he corrected her loudly, his name echoing in a plaintive wail from the bedroom. They both started in that direction, colliding in the doorway. "Is your name Ernie?" he asked pointedly, pushing his way on through. Hannah followed behind him, the frightened call from the bedroom closing around her heart like an icy hand.

Petey was sitting up in the middle of the bed, clutching Cowpoke in her arms. She reached out for Ernie Watson as soon as he cleared the doorway, flinging herself on him when he was close enough.

"Whoa, Pete!" Ernie said, overbalanced onto his bad knee. He held her tightly and walked around the room with her while the little girl sobbed into his shoulder. "You're okay, Pete," he soothed her. "Take it easy, now..." He continued to walk around with her while Hannah helplessly looked on, knowing she didn't have the first idea what to do with a frightened child. For that matter, she didn't know what to do with one who *wasn't* frightened. Ernie glanced at her, hesitating for a moment as if he was going to say something. Then, apparently changing his mind, he walked on. Hannah had never felt so useless in her life.

"Okay, Pete," Ernie said. "A little more crying and then we're through with it, you hear?"

Amazingly, the limit Ernie set seemed to work. Petey sobbed a bit longer, then raised her head. Hannah, finally thinking of *something*, handed him some tissues so he could dry her eyes.

"Are you through crying now?" he asked, gently wiping Petey's eyes.

She nodded solemnly, her mouth puckered and trembling.

"Okay, good—that's my Pete." He tried to sit on the edge of the bed without bending his knee, but he didn't make it, and Hannah winced with him. He reached up and caught her by the wrist so she would sit with them, his fingers strong and warm against the sensitive skin of her inner arm. He didn't let go right away, and he stared into her eyes long enough to unsettle her again. "Now, Pete, right here's your Aunt Hannah. Did you know nobody's given her a special hug and a kiss for a hundred and fifty years? Have they, Miss Hannah?"

"Ah—no," Hannah said in response to the raised eyebrows and his warm squeeze of her wrist. She had no idea what he was talking about, but she was game. "At least that long," she added, trying to be helpful.

"See? Now you're her special niece—the only one

she's got. So I reckon if she's going to get a special hug and kiss, you got to do it, right?"

Hannah frowned. Ernie Watson was making this hug-and-kiss business sound about as desirable as a dose of castor oil.

"Come here, cutie," Hannah said, taking matters into her own hands. She held out her arms, and to her surprise, Petey came into them. They hugged each other tightly and kissed cheeks, Hannah all the while feeling a sudden, ridiculous urge to cry. Her eyes met Ernie Watson's over the top of Petey's head in a look that lingered until she had to glance away. She couldn't tell what he was thinking. She really didn't care what he was thinking, she told herself, but she understood he was trying to make his leaving easier for Petey. "Does she have any clothes with her?" she asked him, trying to sound more capable than she felt.

"Not many. Jeans, mostly, and T-shirts."

"Something to sleep in?"

"No."

Hannah sighed. "Well, Petey, you've got to have a nightie. Let's find you one."

She led Petey to the dresser and pulled open the bottom drawer. "You pick," Hannah told her. "Whichever one you want."

Petey looked up at her doubtfully.

"Go on," Hannah coaxed. "What do you think of this one?" She held up a Mickey Mouse sleep shirt, a Christmas present she'd never worn. But Perrin Marie O'Day was a child after her own heart. She knelt down on the floor and went straight for the frilly stuff, quietly taking each garment out and holding it up.

Hannah sat down on the bed again, forgetting in her

pleasure at Petey's delight with lace and satin that her intimate apparel was being systematically exposed to Ernie Watson's full view. "She doesn't say much, does she?" she observed. She turned her head to look at him. He was engrossed in studying the black lace nightgown with the slit up the front, which Petey was trying to unfurl.

"No," Ernie said, his voice sounding a bit strange. He was soft-spoken anyway. He had the kind of voice that would soothe upset children, and horses, and women, but with that one word, he sounded as if he wasn't getting enough air. He swallowed hard before he went on. "What you heard her say when I put her down in here was the most she'd come up with all day— damn," Ernie commented under his breath as Petey held up a particularly flimsy white silk and lacy teddy. "I got to get out of here," he decided, abruptly standing up, bad knee or no bad knee.

"Ernie!" Petey cried, the lingerie drawer forgotten.

"Pete, we talked about this," he said firmly, bending down to pick her up. "You know I got to get my knee fixed, and I got to get to the rodeo in Rapid City."

Her bottom lip was trembling again.

"Now, what did I tell you I'd do when I got there?" he asked.

"Call me on the—phone," Petey managed.

"That's right. Give me a big hug." He paused while Petey hugged him. "I'll call you on the phone. And I want you and Cowpoke to behave yourselves and look after Miss Hannah here. You take her to the grocery store and show her what to buy and make her eat right."

"Green vegetables," Petey said.

"Right! Green vegetables. Milk and fruit—no junk.

And none of that carton cereal with all the sugar in it. Okay?"

She didn't answer.

"Okay?" he repeated.

This time she nodded, pushing against him to get down and go back to the lingerie drawer. He patted her on the head and picked up the cowboy hat Hannah had left on the foot of the bed. He looked at Petey for a moment, then limped out of the room with Hannah following behind him.

"Are you going to telephone her?" she asked when they reached the front door.

"I said I would," he answered shortly.

"You might like the phone number, then. As you know, it's not in the book."

He was about to say something but didn't, pressing his lips together and hooking his thumbs in his jeans pockets while she wrote the number down on a notepad and tore off the sheet. He stuck it in his shirt pocket without looking at it.

"Do you need money?" he asked bluntly. "I can let you have—"

"No, I don't need money," Hannah interrupted. At least she didn't need his.

"I was just asking, Hannah. You're not working at a major network television station anymore. The place you're at now ain't exactly big time."

"I don't need money," she repeated, wondering how the devil he knew anything about that.

He smiled, clearly enjoying her annoyance. "Right. Well, I can't say this hasn't been interesting." He opened the door, his eyes searching hers for a moment, until she purposefully looked away. Whatever he was up to, she was *not* responding to it.

"Don't forget to call Petey," she said, because she couldn't keep from saying it. He didn't make any sense to her at all. First, he'd wanted to dump Petey as quickly as possible, then he didn't think she was fit to look after her, and now he was once again hell-bent on leaving. The sudden mental picture of Petey hovering around a telephone that didn't ring was something she didn't want to think about.

"I'll call the kid, Hannah. Her clothes are in that bag over there." He nodded toward a grocery bag, which sat on the couch. "I brought them in when I brought the bear. You better keep up with the bear. She gets upset without it—especially at night."

Hannah, still waiting for him to go, didn't say anything.

He sighed and put on his hat. Clearly, he really wasn't sure about doing this.

"I'll . . . take good care of her," Hannah offered. "Thank you for bringing her."

"Yeah," he said, then grinned. "Thank *you* for helping me get out of my pants. So. Good-bye, Miss Hannah." He sighed again and finally went out the door, but he caught hold of it at the last moment to keep her from closing it. She waited for him to say whatever he was going to say, but he didn't say anything. She could tell he wanted to, and that was making her all . . . addled again. She could feel the rise in her pulse, the warm flush of her cheeks. It was as if they had come to the moment that would decide whether either of them acknowledged—albeit tentatively—the mutual interest they were feeling or whether they would just be sensible and let it go.

Hannah lowered her eyes to the open neck of his plaid shirt. Beneath it he was wearing one of those old-fashioned undershirts with the buttons at the neck, buttons that weren't fastened, letting her see the beginnings of the dark, curling hair on his chest. If anyone—if *she* happened to press her face there, she'd smell that heady masculine scent of his, the soap and the leather and the—

"Hannah?"

"What?" she said guiltily, her eyes flying to his as if she thought he could somehow tell what she'd been thinking. What was the matter with her?

"You're a good sport, Miss Hannah," he said, his soft voice gently teasing.

"I don't think it counts if you don't have a choice," she answered.

"Yeah, it counts. You're a good sport—but you don't take any crap."

Hannah frowned, wondering why in the world that sounded like a compliment, and why it pleased her so that it did.

"You don't look like Libby," he added quietly, and she suddenly had the wild notion that he wanted to touch her. It was because of the trouble he'd just brought to Elizabeth's sister, she assured herself. Nothing more. She stood there, incredulous at the delicious anticipation that suffused her body as she imagined the warm, rough hand that had comforted Petey reaching up to lightly touch her face.

"I know," she said abruptly, attempting to close the door again before he actually did touch her. Because her heart was pounding, because she was getting another feeling—one she had no business getting, a feeling more dangerous than the one she'd had when he'd done his masculine appraisal of her sweat suit, a feeling that was dark and warm and growing stronger the longer she let him look into her eyes.

"Hannah?"

"What?" she said again. It took a lot of effort to say it, and she couldn't have looked away from those dark eyes of his if her life had depended on it.

"I'm glad."

CHAPTER TWO

HANNAH SAT in the dark wishing she had some vice for comfort. She didn't smoke; she didn't drink. She had nothing to put between her and her worry but a cup of lemon zinger herbal tea. It wasn't helping. It was three o'clock in the morning and raining hard. Petey had awakened twice already with nightmares, and Hannah hadn't been able to sleep even before that. Having a restless four-year-old in one's bed was like sleeping with a performing acrobat—while he performed.

Hannah moved from the kitchen table to an easy chair by the window in the living room, opening the drapes and looking out into the rain-wet parking lot. The streetlight outside caused the rivulets of rain on the windowpane to cast strange, mottled shadows on her hands and arms. She lived in an older apartment complex, one with the living space actually cut up into rooms, and one having real six-over-six sash windows that were anything but energy efficient, but were aesthetically pleasing. She lived here because she could afford it and because she liked the solid feel these older places had. So what was she going to do about the No Children clause? Ignore it in the hope that Elizabeth would turn up soon? Hide Petey from the neighbors? Except for the nightmares, Petey didn't seem likely to make enough noise to cause comment.

Poor Petey, dressed in Hannah's pink satin sleep shirt and a matching short robe. The outfit had swallowed her whole, but Hannah had never seen a child so pleased. She'd looked at herself in the mirror for a long time, turning this way and that. And her primary concern had been to show it to John Ernest Watson, who was long gone and likely to stay that way. Hannah pictured him driving on the rainswept interstate even now, determined to get to the rodeo in Rapid City, whether he could walk without limping or get his own pants off or not.

Ernie. He wasn't the first person to note that she looked nothing like Elizabeth, but he was the first one to make such a kind comment.

I'm glad.

Two insignificant words, and she couldn't stop thinking about him. Remembering the way he'd said it gave her that dark, warm feeling again, and yet she knew exactly what he'd meant. After all that Elizabeth had apparently put him through over the years, he was relieved not to have to deal with someone who looked like her. It had to have been that. What else could it have been? He hadn't meant he was glad because he was attracted to *her*. Elizabeth was ... Elizabeth; she was only Hannah.

She sighed and wondered if he and Elizabeth had been lovers, recognizing a nagging and inappropriate hope that they hadn't been, which was ridiculous. Of course, they had been—regardless of the way he'd looked at her with those eyes of his, eyes that had made her want to comfort him or bandage his knee or whatever else he needed, even though she'd only just met him. And they'd hardly gotten off on the right foot. He had thought she was some kind of anorexic, career-minded nitwit who knew nothing about mothering. She thought he was ...

She wasn't quite sure what she thought he was. Kind to small children, certainly, and dangerously appealing. One of those charming, irrepressible, macho types indigenous to cowboy country, who were annoyingly overprotective of women as long as it didn't interfere with their nights out with the boys. And probably still in love with Elizabeth. A man wouldn't have inconvenienced himself the way he had otherwise; there had to be more between Elizabeth and him than nostalgia for childhood, though Elizabeth had never said so. She had always been candid about such things, discussing her current bedmate as easily as someone else might have given the time of day. But Elizabeth, who was always "in love," had never mentioned John Ernest Watson in that respect. She'd never mentioned that he had been a husband candidate or that she had broken his heart. The mental picture of his rough, weathered hands gently wiping away Petey's tears and his dark eyes once again finding hers over Petey's head suddenly came to mind. In his tenderness to Petey, he had shown he cared about

Elizabeth a great deal. And he was sad because his love didn't matter to her.

So there you are, Hannah Rose. There were all the reasons why she shouldn't even be thinking about Ernie Watson, much less letting herself feel anything for him. She wasn't going to see him again anyway. She sighed and finished her tea and another pitiful wail came from the bedroom—Ernie Watson's name. *Ah, Petey,* she thought, feeling her way toward the sound. *The last thing you want to do is love a rodeo man.* She had been in Texas long enough to know they were as bad as baseball players in gold neck chains or oil field wildcatters. They were fun for the moment, but a woman couldn't count on them to be there when she needed them.

She was able to settle Petey down with minimal difficulty this time; the child just seemed to need to know she hadn't been left alone, that someone to whom she belonged was nearby. Hannah wondered if Elizabeth had ever done this before. And why hadn't she left Petey with her father? Or with her grandfather, for heaven's sake? No, Elizabeth had to upend two totally uninvolved people's lives—hers and Ernie Watson's—in typical "Libby" fashion.

Petey slept through until morning. She was still asleep when Hannah called the television station to let them know she wouldn't be in. When she told the station manager exactly what her problem was, he was understanding enough—because Ernie Watson had been there the night before trying to locate her, and because she had the scripts for the furniture outlet commercials she'd been working on, which she promised to finish at home. And she had every intention of doing so—ignorant as she was of what it was like to have a four-year-old underfoot, whether she had a spangled bear to comfort her or not. Petey had started talking more, but Hannah's biggest aggravation was Petey and the telephone. She constantly picked up the receiver to see if Ernie was there when Hannah wasn't looking; then she'd leave it off the hook until the alert signal sounded.

"No, Petey," Hannah said, trying to be patient. "Ernie can't call you unless the phone is just like this— see? Don't pick it up." She gave up after the thousandth interruption, taking Petey and herself and the bear out into the rain to the grocery store before they drove each other entirely crazy. They had gotten by on peanut butter toast and Tang for breakfast, but, as Ernie Watson had so tactlessly pointed out, the cupboard was nearly bare.

"Rules," Hannah said before they went inside. "First and foremost: No talking to strangers. Number two: Stick to me like glue. And absolutely, positively no taking anything off the shelf without my expressed permission. Understand?"

"Yes," Petey said sweetly. And she understood all right; she just wasn't going to do it.

"Petey!" Hannah said in exasperation the third time she tried to sneak a giant bag of marshmallows into the cart.

"I think these are a green vegetable," Petey said hopefully.

"No way," Hannah said, fighting down a grin. "Put those back—right now."

Petey complied, but only because Hannah was using her producer's voice, the same one she used on lackadaisical cameramen when she was trying to get a commercial finished. Well, she'd always said cameramen were absolute children.

She returned from the grocery store with nothing but

nutritious things to eat, a severely diminished check-book balance, and a grave case of total exhaustion. She barely had the strength to put the groceries away. *My God, how do women with more than one child do this?* She felt nothing but admiration for the mothers she'd seen grocery shopping while they pushed one child and led two others. When she'd finished, she collapsed on the living room couch with her feet propped up on the coffee table—just a little rest before she tried again to work on the commercials.

"Aunt Hannah?" Petey said, sitting down beside her and trying to prop her feet up, too. The "t" was some-how lost in her pronunciation of Hannah's now well-used title, making her name sound like Anna-Hannah.

"My dear, sweet Petey, what?" Hannah said, know-ing that Petey would grin. She did, and Hannah grinned with her. She rather liked this little kid, whether she could get her commercial script done or not.

"Tie my shoe, please."

"Again?" Hannah said in mock horror, making Petey give another smile. "Foot, please." Petey stuck a sneaker up for Hannah's attention.

The shoe had really seen better days, Hannah noticed while she retied. "Are you tired?" she asked.

"I don't want to take a nap," Petey advised her, cut-ting through to what she thought was the real reason for the inquiry about her state of fatigue.

"Good. Do you think we could go out in the rain again and buy you some new shoes?"

"You got to fix the 'mercial," Petey said.

"Shoes first, then I fix the 'mercial, okay?"

"Okay," Petey said, convinced.

Hannah's apartment complex was located south of the Trinity River, which translated to Below the Salt to the upwardly mobile movers and shakers of Dallas. She took Petey into north Dallas to the elite Galleria mall so she could see the ice skaters. They had two hours of that and shopping for a pair of expensive running shoes with Velcro closings, assorted frilly little-girl things, a yellow poncho, and ice cream. They returned home in a downpour, which didn't penetrate the new poncho, but which was certainly going to wet the newly shod feet. Hannah wore herself out trying to carry Petey and Cowpoke over the puddles, manage the umbrella, and hang on to her packages.

"Oh, I'm sorry!" she said to the innocent bystander she plowed into because she couldn't see around the umbrella.

"Well, if it's not Sneaky Pete and Miss Hannah," Ernie Watson said. He took the umbrella out of her hand, holding it up high enough to clear his cowboy hat and putting his arm around her to keep both her and Petey dry. Hannah found herself nearly nose to nose with him and unable to do anything about it because Petey had locked her free arm around his neck.

Oh, God, Hannah thought immediately and with some dismay. *I'm glad to see him.* She wasn't supposed to be glad to see him. She'd convinced herself sometime before dawn that whatever had passed between them had been nothing—even if it was something. Worse, she suspected he was glad to see her, too, and just about as thrilled with the situation as she was. His tired eyes swept over her face. She was close enough to tell that he hadn't been drinking, and she suspected he still hadn't had much sleep.

"You've got freckles," he noted, his dark eyes more rascally than sad at that particular moment.

Hannah frowned. His proximity and his clean male

scent were calling up that dark, warm feeling again. Lord, what a nice face he had. Nice face, nice thighs . . .

"Yes, I know," she said dryly, trying not to return the mischievous grin she was getting. "Petey and I are lucky that way."

"I got new shoes," Petey offered.

"Yeah? Stick your foot up here and let me see."

Petey did it gladly, nearly overbalancing them all into the shrubbery.

"Well, dang if you don't," Ernie observed. "Fine-looking shoes, they are, too. Who bought you those?"

"Anna-Hannah. We don't got money, but we got plastic."

"You don't say," he answered, casting a look at Hannah apparently because of Petey's talkativeness. "That was nice. Did you say thank you?"

"Nope."

"Well, somebody around here better say it before they end up on my list," he said, giving Hannah a wink.

"What are you doing here? I thought you were going to South Dakota," Hannah said, ignoring the wink and hoping to uncover some reason that would negate her pleasure at seeing him.

"So did I. I got to thinking about the kid—"

"We're doing all right," she interrupted.

"—and you," he finished.

And me? she almost said, the dark, warm feeling spreading, making her knees weak, making her heart pound. Once again his dark eyes traveled over her face. He really didn't seem to mind that she was only Hannah or that she had freckles or that her eating habits were less than nutritionally sound. And here she was standing in the pouring rain behaving like a fool! "You didn't have to come back," she said with as much conviction as she could muster.

"Yeah, that's what I told myself the whole time I was getting my knee patched up and all the way down I-35 —in both directions." He started them walking toward Hannah's doorstep. "Somehow I just couldn't make myself believe it. You going to let me come in out of the rain?" he asked when Hannah would have taken exception to his lack of faith in her child-care abilities.

"Depends on whether or not you're going to make me take your pants off," she said pointedly. She intended to be sarcastic, but she only made him grin that teasing, mischievous grin.

"Nope. The doc closed the cut with clamps so I could bend my knee a little . . . unless, of course, you *want* to take my pants off."

A discreet little cough sounded and Hannah looked around directly into Rick Archer's eyes. Her first inclination was to get out of Ernie's embrace, but since neither he nor Petey seemed to have any intention of letting go of what they had, she simply stood.

"I thought that was you," Rick said, his voice as tight as the small frown fixed just between his eyes. "So what's going on?" His eyes cut to Ernie Watson and back again. "You weren't at work today. Nobody at KHRB seemed to know why."

"I had a family problem," Hannah said, not liking the accusation in his voice. She had been out with him a number of times, but not enough to justify the annoyance she was hearing now. They weren't lovers— though they had come close once, before Hannah had come to her senses. She liked Rick; he was witty and ruggedly handsome and fun, but she simply hadn't wanted that kind of involvement. She was troubled by his keen ambition, for one thing. He had his own local talk show, *People's Eye,* and had every hope of one day receiving the "call" from one of the networks, no matter what he had to do to get it. She had let ambition take over her own life once, as balm for a broken heart, and to a very unadmirable end. She'd become jaded and callous, until she'd finally realized that she didn't want success at the price of her self-respect—either for herself or for Rick, whom she liked and wanted to respect.

"I didn't know you had cowboys in the family," he said lightly, his eyes flicking over Ernie in a way that would have made a lesser man self-conscious. The look seemed to have no effect on Ernie at all.

"John Ernest Watson," Ernie said before Hannah could make any introductions. He handed the umbrella to Petey so he could shake hands. Petey promptly clunked Rick in the head with it. "I'm a friend of Hannah's sister, Elizabeth," Ernie added, trying not to grin.

"Frederick Archer," Rick said, dodging another of Petey's passes with the umbrella. "I'm a friend of Hannah's."

Hannah listened to this subtle male parry with fascination. Underlying the seemingly innocent social exchange was what amounted to, if not the actual drawing of swords, a certain hand-on-the-scabbard warning—when neither one of them had any right whatsoever to draw territorial boundaries where she was concerned.

"Rick, would you open the door for us?" Hannah said, managing to pass him her keys. He opened the door, and, still limping, Ernie took Petey inside, pausing long enough to let her get her packages from Hannah before he carried her into the kitchen. "Be sure you show him the refrigerator, Petey," Hannah called after them, her eyes meeting Ernie's in a look she couldn't read as he discreetly closed the door.

"So what's going on?" Rick said immediately.

"A lot," she answered. "And then some." She sat down on the sofa and tried to massage into oblivion the headache she'd picked up somewhere along the way. Lord, what she'd give for a nap. She suddenly smiled, hearing Petey in the kitchen explaining something about green vegetables.

"Well?" Rick said after a moment. "Are you going to tell me what's going on or not?"

She looked at him sharply. He was using that tone of voice again.

"My sister left her little girl, Petey, with Ernie—"

"Ernie who?"

"John Ernest Watson, the man you just met!" Hannah snapped because her head hurt and because he was venting his annoyance by pretending to be obtuse. He was a talk show host; he wasn't *that* dense. "Ernie brought Petey to me. Neither of us has any idea where Elizabeth is or when she's coming back or what this is all about. None." She glanced at him. He seemed to be waiting for the punch line.

"Oh," he said when she didn't go on. "So how long have you known this . . . Ernie?"

"Eighteen hours," she said evenly.

He smiled and tugged at a strand of her hair. "Want to go someplace tonight?"

"I can't." She wondered if he'd been listening at all.

"Why not?"

"I don't have a baby-sitter," she said, realizing for the first time, after years of hearing her friends and co-workers say those very same words, what an impact they had.

"You mean the kid's staying here?" he said incredulously.

"Yes, of course she's staying here. What did you think—"

"For how long?" he interrupted.

"Rick, I don't know. I just told you: Elizabeth's gone."

"And you're going to keep her daughter until she comes back? Hannah, there are agencies that take care of this sort of thing."

"Just what kind of agency did you have in mind, Rick? The pound?"

"The Department of Social Services, for openers. Hannah, you can't keep her."

"Why can't I? I'm her aunt."

"Have you got her birth certificate and immunization records?" he interrupted again, his annoyance showing now.

"No. What has that got to do with anything?"

"Well, if you want her in good day care—and I assume you do—you have to prove how old she is, you need proof that she's been immunized. If she hasn't got any records, she'll have to have all the shots over again, and she can't have them unless her parent or guardian gives permission. You aren't her parent or her guardian. You see the problem? And what if she gets sick or hurt? You can't give permission for anything she might need. How are you going to work unless you can get her into day care? You might find a private individual to keep her, but that's expensive. You took a big pay cut when you came to KHRB."

"How do you know so much about this?" she said, feeling like the half-wit Ernie thought she was. She hadn't considered any of these things.

"On *People's Eye* I do something about child care almost every week. You'll have to have her declared a ward of the court and then file a petition for guardianship—"

"I'm not going to do that!"

"Well, what else can you do, Hannah? Who's going to keep her for you?"

"I am," Ernie said from the doorway, and his frown told Hannah he'd been listening for quite a while. "I'm supposed to stay away from bull chasing for ten days," he said to Hannah. "I was planning to hang around Dallas anyway. I'll keep Petey for you."

"You can't do that," Hannah said, because she knew he didn't want to, and he certainly didn't have to.

"Sure I can. You know she'd be all right with me."

"I know, but—"

"I don't see there's much choice, Hannah—with the mess Libby's left you in. I can do it for ten days or so. That'll give you time to decide what to do if Libby's not back by then." His eyes held hers. Kind eyes, understanding eyes, eyes that made her want to do something silly like cry or fall at his feet in gratitude and hug his knees—knee.

"Ernie, I don't know what to say." She was telling the truth. She didn't. And she couldn't keep from looking at him, all of him. He smiled—not the mischievous smile she'd been getting, but one that was gentle and a little shy. She was seeing the real John Ernest Watson at that moment, she thought, not the hell-raising womanizer Elizabeth had described, not the rodeo clown, and not the rascal who blithely took his pants off in strange women's bathrooms.

"Well, now, this is cozy," Rick said, his talk-show-host sarcasm intact.

"What this is," Ernie said quietly, "is none of your business."

"Yeah, right," Rick said. "None of my business. You keep the kid for Hannah, and she'll take your pants off for you."

"I'd watch my mouth if I were you."

"Oh, please," Rick said, holding up both hands. "Spare me the Gene Autry Cowboy Code of Honor fisticuffs." He got up and headed for the door. "Hannah? It's been fun. Be seeing you around."

"Rick—" Hannah protested, but he didn't stop, slamming the door hard on his way out.

CHAPTER THREE

THE SILENCE IN the room grew long and heavy, broken only by the sound of the rain against the windows and Petey's singsong rendition of "Honky Tonk Man" in the kitchen. Hannah tried to smile, knowing she wouldn't have to look far to discover just who had taught it to her. Her beloved Ernie, who was probably just like the man in the song, devoted to drinking and gambling and wild women, and begging to come home to the poor woman who loved him, only when his money ran out.

Lord, she shouldn't be feeling the things she was feeling about him, much less considering his offer of child care! He was watching her closely, as if he expected her to cry over Rick's dramatic departure. But

Rick was the last thing on her mind, and damn it all, what choice did she have?

She finally looked up at him. He was standing with his thumbs hooked in his jeans pockets and his hat shoved to the back of his head. He hobbled over to the couch and sat down beside her—not such a good idea since he couldn't do it without stressing his injured knee. Hannah instinctively put her hand on his bare forearm to steady him, and that wasn't such a good idea, either. She was perfectly aware she had no business touching him and the feel of his warm, muscular arm beneath her fingers was nearly her undoing. She quickly took her hand away.

If I just stay away from him, it'll be all right, she promised herself. She even halfway believed it. Anyway, it was just for a day or two, until she could think of something else. "Ernie—"

"You okay?" he interrupted, his voice as gentle with her as it had been with Petey when she'd had her nightmare.

"Ernie—"

"I'm . . . sorry about your boyfriend, Hannah. I could talk to him if you want, explain to him how you happened to take my pants off."

"Ernie—"

"I don't think he'll stay mad long, Hannah. And you can't blame him. When a man thinks his woman is taking off somebody else's pants—"

"Ernie!"

"What?" he said finally, his face breaking into a grin.

"Could you take care of Petey now? I've got to finish some scripts for a furniture-outlet commercial, and I have to monitor an adult reading class at the library. It's part of a KHRB public service project, and those people will be waiting for me. I *have* to be there." She was uncomfortable enough to be rattled, television background or not, but he'd made the offer, and she *needed* him, God help her, no matter how dangerous he was.

He smiled, but he was looking at her curiously. "You're not one to cry over spilt milk, are you?"

"No, and I don't look a gift horse in the mouth, either. Rick is . . . upset, because he'd rather be upset than have to deal with a woman who has a problem. Can you take care of Petey for me now or not?"

"You got it, Miss Hannah. We'll stay out of your way until you get what you need to do finished."

"There's just one thing—"

"I've been on the wagon for twenty-two months and ten days, Hannah. If the time comes when I think I can't make it any longer, I'll bring Petey to you," he said, anticipating her question and looking her in the eye. "And I've got to say just one thing of my own."

"What?"

"I'll look after Petey so you can work, but that's all. I'm not taking her off your hands so you can run around with Roderick."

"Frederick," Hannah corrected. "And I don't *run around*—with him or anybody else."

"Just so we understand each other."

"Oh, I think we understand each other," Hannah said. Neither of them wanted any more trouble.

"Now, why does that make you mad?"

"It doesn't," she lied, and she was careful not to make eye contact. The comment did make her angry, because he assumed she was like Elizabeth. She wasn't. She was herself. And it was disturbing to her how much she wanted him to know it. "I'll check around so I'll know how much to pay you—"

"Now, that's another thing," he interrupted. "It's not going to do for us to keep offering each other money. It's kind of crazy when you think about it—when two people are as poor as we are."

She tried not to smile, but didn't quite make it. "I'll pay you," she said firmly when she had her face under control. It was the only way she could justify doing this. She glanced at him. He was looking at her—a bit tolerantly, she thought. The same sort of look he might give Petey when her ambitions exceeded her capabilities. Well, she meant what she said. She might have to pay him in installments, but she would pay him.

"Miss Hannah, what am I going to do with you?"

"Nothing," she said shortly, getting up from the couch.

"How about a little help," Ernie said, holding out his hand to her.

She hesitated, knowing she'd have to take both his hands to get him standing. Her small hands were lost in the warm roughness of his big ones, and the contact only served to verify what she already knew: She must be out of her mind. This infatuation of hers was going to give her nothing but grief, and Lord knew, she already had enough of that.

Ernie was as good as his word, keeping Petey in the living room watching television while Hannah worked diligently at the kitchen table. Her mind kept wandering as she listened to their conversation. He really was good with Petey—firm, but kind. She couldn't keep from smiling at the enthusiasm with which the two of them watched a *Dukes of Hazzard* rerun. It was hard to tell sometimes which sound effects came with the show and which were supplied by Ernie and Petey. She left for the library at seven, surprised that she would really rather have stayed and watched sitcom reruns with her niece and her impromptu baby-sitter. It was well after nine when she returned. She came back to an empty apartment, fighting the panic until she found a note telling her that they had taken her extra door key and gone to McDonald's for milk shakes. She went to work again at the kitchen table, hearing them when they returned. But they didn't seem to require anything from her, and she forced herself to keep working, finishing the scripts shortly before midnight. She was satisfied with the result, but God, she was tired. She looked up to find Ernie standing in the kitchen doorway.

"How's it going?" he asked.

"Fine. I'm finished. Thanks, Ernie. I'll take over with Petey now." *Somehow.*

"No, she's asleep. Has been for a long time. You stay where you are."

"Why?" she asked as he limped into the kitchen, her first dreaded thought that he had another session of first aid planned. She couldn't even cope with touching his bare arm; she'd never manage his bare knee.

"You got to eat, Miss Hannah. I told you that last night. I haven't had anything to eat since that brown milk shake, so I'm going to whip us up something."

"Whip away," Hannah said in relief. She had groceries now, and she was too tired for false courtesy. If he wanted to cook, he could cook. "A brown milk shake?" it suddenly occurred to her to ask.

"That's what Petey ordered for us at McDonald's: two brown milk shakes." He raised and lowered his eyebrows once, and Hannah smiled in spite of herself. What a nice man he was, she thought in dismay. Handsome, beautiful sad eyes, kind to small children, and nice for goodness' sake.

He made Spanish omelets and coffee while she watched. Admittedly, she was more interested in the cook than in the cuisine, and her eyes followed him constantly, as if something he did or didn't do was going to tell her the real reason why he'd come back to Dallas. Not that she didn't already know the real reason —his regard for Elizabeth. She noted that he worked quickly, in spite of having to limp around the kitchen, and that he had other injuries, old injuries: a crooked little finger on his left hand, scars on the bridge of his nose and in the middle of his chin. He looked up once, she thought because he felt her staring at him, but he didn't say anything, giving her a sassy wink and going back to what he was doing with only a brief thoughtful glance. The eggs were delicious, and she ate with more zest than she had in some time, both because she had finished the scripts and because she was quite frankly enjoying the company of the cook.

"This is wonderful," she said. "Where did you learn to do this?" It was hard for her to accept such incongruous talent in a rodeo clown.

"Here and there," he answered vaguely.

"Ah," she said. "Some woman taught you, right?"

He gave her his well-rehearsed mischievous grin and didn't answer.

"So," she said. "How did you get to be a rodeo clown?"

"Just kind of fell into it, I guess. I started rodeoing when I was a kid. I was pretty good at it—got to be Best All Around Cowboy once. And then one day they were short a clown, so I figured I'd give it a whirl. I was young and crazy then," he added with a pleasant little chuckle she hadn't heard before. "Now I'm just crazy."

"Go on," Hannah said, smiling in return.

"Well, I liked it. I like"—he paused to find the right way to say it—"keeping a man from getting hurt if I can. It makes you feel good when some cowboy comes up to you and shakes your hand and tells you he appreciates what you did for him out in the arena." He stared too long into her eyes, and Hannah was the first to look away.

"Do you have children?" she asked next, feeling an intense need for conversation. She had to do something. She was so aware of him she could hardly stand it.

"No," he answered. Period.

"Then how do you know so much about them?"

"I don't. I like kids. They like me. You get to meet a lot of kids when you're a rodeo clown. And I'm a god-father."

"You're a godfather?" She didn't mean to sound so incredulous, but somehow, as good with Petey as he was, he was still supposed to be a hard-drinking wo-manizer—not a likely choice for a godparent.

"I have two god-children," he said in the same tone of voice. "A little boy and a little girl. The boy's name is Adam McDade—he's five. His sister's name is Cissy. She's almost two. They live in Chimayo, New Mexico. Their father, Mac, and I have been friends since we were boys." He smiled and looked her directly in the eye. "I know it's crazy for people like Mac and his wife Amelia—and Libby—and *you*—to go around trusting me to take care of their kids. But they do. What can I say?"

"I didn't mean—"

"Yes, you did."

Hannah looked down at her plate. She'd hurt his feelings, and she hadn't meant to do that. The silence lengthened, and the eggs she'd been enjoying weren't so enjoyable anymore.

"So," Ernie said after what seemed a long time. "Did you get fired from the big station downtown or what?"

She looked up at him sharply, thinking he wanted to pick a fight because she'd insulted him. She still thought so, in spite of his grin. "No, I didn't get fired from the big station downtown. Do you always ask exactly what you want to know?"

"Always," he assured her. "I move around a lot. I don't have the time to waste on working up to something. So why did you leave?" he persisted, pouring her another cup of coffee without asking. He made excellent coffee, too, Hannah noted.

"I've moved around a lot myself, but a little tact is never amiss."

"So why did you leave?" he asked again, ignoring her pointed observation. His eyes studied hers, making her feel as if there were things he wanted to know about her, things he *would* know, regardless of what she said or did.

"I had a moment of truth and saw myself as a despicable person," she answered shortly, getting back to her omelet.

"Yeah? I had one of those, too. That's when I quit drinking. Kind of like Saul-on-the-road-to-Tarsus, aren't they? So where was yours?"

"None of your business, Watson." She was finding conversation wasn't such a good idea after all.

"I don't know what that's got to do with anything. If I waited around for things that were my business, Petey and I wouldn't be here. She'd be in a foster home someplace, and I'd be in South Dakota. Go on. Tell me. I'm not going to think badly of you."

"I don't care if you think badly of me or not!" she said, knowing she just didn't want him to think she was anything like Elizabeth.

He grinned. "Then tell me. Where was it?"

"In the Dallas airport!" she said in exasperation. His grin widened, but there was something in his eyes that suddenly lessened her annoyance—empathy, she supposed. "It was . . . after an airliner crashed. My cameraman and I were one of the first news teams to get there. They wouldn't let us out to the crash scene, so we worked the airport. People . . . were coming in. People who didn't know if their family and friends were on the plane that had crashed on takeoff. We dogged them through the airport—really great pictures, you know?

"You have to get great pictures because that guarantees you a spot on the six o'clock news—maybe a chance to be picked up by the network. And if you're in the news business you want to get picked up by the network. A few good spots today, and you're an anchor somewhere tomorrow." She stopped, because she'd never spoken about the real reasons for her resignation to anyone. She looked at him across the table, again noting how at ease she felt talking to him. She didn't know what it was about him that made her let her guard down the way she did. Maybe it was because he seemed to be so open about things—about some things, at least.

"Go on," Ernie said quietly. She wanted to look away from him, and she couldn't. And she wanted to tell him.

"It . . . suddenly hit me—what I was doing. These were real people—frightened people anticipating the worst tragedy they could imagine, and I was there feeding off their fear in the name of 'news.' It was disgusting. *I* was disgusting. So I left." She gave a small shrug and finally looked away. She didn't mention the man she'd loved when she was in her twenties, the man whose leaving had driven her to that kind of mindless worship of her career.

"And you like what you're doing now?"

She gave a small smile. "Ever see the Big Bob Bowzer furniture outlet commercial on KHRB-TV?"

"With Big Bob dressed like a cross between a ballerina and Tinker Bell?"

"Right—flesh-colored bodysuit, silver tutu, wings, and a wand—and he flits around the store from bargain to bargain. I wrote that commercial. Since Bowzer started airing it, his sales have gone up six-point-eight percent."

He laughed that soft, chuckling laugh again, the one that he probably didn't use much, but that sounded sincere when he did. "I know Bob Bowzer," he said. "How the devil did you get him to do that?"

"It wasn't hard. He likes to be silly."

"And letting Big Bob be silly is better than aiming for an anchor job with the network?"

"Well, it beats standing in the rain in a yellow poncho telling people it's raining and praying lightning doesn't run in on your mike before you can tell them. I started in this business as a high school student—a volunteer gofer. I did a little bit of everything, learned it from the ground up. Now I'm doing a little bit of everything again—producing, directing, writing. Sometimes I even sweep. It . . . really is better. You know how they introduced me at the reading class tonight? As the person who turned Big Bob Bowzer into a fairy—Ernie, why are you doing this?" she asked abruptly. She didn't want to avoid the issue any longer. She was attracted to him, and she was certain he knew it. She'd save herself

a lot of trouble and heartache if he'd just say it. I'm here
because I'm still in love with Elizabeth.

"Doing what?" he asked, looking down and pushing
his eggs around his plate with a very suspicious noncha-
lance.

"Don't. Please. You know what. You said you
weren't getting mixed up with any more Browne
women."

"Yeah, I said that," he admitted. He looked up at her,
his expression unreadable.

"Then what are you doing here?"

He put down his fork and braced his arms on the
edge of the table. "I thought you didn't look a gift horse
in the mouth."

"Once a newsperson, always a newsperson. Tell me.
I want to know."

"I told you. I came back because of Petey. And because of you."

"Me," Hannah repeated. "Because you think I won't
take good care of her."

"No, because I don't mind helping you. I told you.
You're a good sport, Hannah—but you don't take any
crap. Men just naturally know how to do that, but it's a
hard thing to find in a woman. And when I left last
night, you looked kind of bewildered . . . sort of like
Bambi when the woods caught on fire. And . . ." He
paused, then grinned. "You got the damnedest drawerful
of underwear it's ever been my privilege to review." He
waggled his eyebrows at her.

"Ernie," Hannah said, trying hard to be serious and
not respond to his flagrant teasing. "Those are the
dumbest reasons I've ever heard."

There it was again. That chuckle she liked so much,
and she laughed with him, enjoying herself, enjoying

him, realizing how relieved she was that she'd given him the chance to put Elizabeth firmly between them—and he hadn't taken it.

"There's more," he said, his smile sliding away so that he was staring at her gravely.

"What?" she asked, her relief short-lived. Now he would tell her.

"I want to see—" He stopped.

"What?" she said again, but he abruptly got up from the table.

"Nothing. I've been awake too damn long. What time do you go into work in the morning?"

"Wait—I thought you didn't waste time working up to things."

"I don't. I ask what I want to ask, but I don't tell what I don't want to tell. What time?"

"Seven o'clock. What were you going to say?" she persisted. She needed to hear the truth from him to keep from making a fool of herself.

" 'Night, Miss Hannah," he said, clearly not planning to answer. "You get to do the dishes. I'll see you in the morning."

"Ernie," she protested, but he kept going.

"I'll see you in the morning," he called over his shoulder.

"Bambi?" she suddenly remembered as the front door slammed.

She didn't expect him to be there. She got up early and dressed, leaving Petey asleep and fully expecting she'd have to call the station manager again with another tale of woe. She paced and watched out the window and waited, feeling the cold fist of anxiety in the pit of her stomach.

Ralax, Hannah, she told herself. *You've got the scripts done, at least.*

Ernie Watson wasn't dependable. Whatever had made her think he was dependable? she asked herself a hundred times. But he arrived on time, freshly showered and looking rather boyish and adorable with his hair wet and slicked down, though he still had his five-o'clock shadow. He gave her his and Petey's itinerary for the day, in case she needed to get in touch with him, and he said a kind word about the way she looked before she left.

She accepted the compliment a bit skeptically— since she was wearing a gray pin-striped business suit and high heels, her hair in a severe bun and a briefcase under her arm. "Thanks a lot, Ernie. You really know how to shore up a woman's confidence."

"Why are you dressed like that?"

"Because I'm selling another furniture outlet commercial. This owner is *not* the Tinker Bell type. I have to look as if I know what I'm doing."

"Well, Hannah, you look like Perry Mason," he advised her.

"I thought I looked like Bambi," she said, searching for the car keys she'd had only a moment ago.

"That's when you're worried. Hey," he said, catching her by the shoulders so he could see her face. The feel of his big warm hands through the fabric of her suit was distracting enough to make her frown. "You're worried again. Now what are you worried about?"

"What am I worried about? Ernie, for heaven's sake!" she said in exasperation. She tried to get away from him. Personal contact with this man was an indulgence she couldn't afford—although the fact that he was a hard-drinking cowboy-womanizer who wouldn't admit that he was in love with her sister ought to be enough deterrent for anyone.

"I mean, besides Elizabeth and Petey, and having to leave Petey with me," he said. The dark eyes that held hers demanded honesty, whether she wanted to give it or not.

"That . . . pretty well covers it," she said, giving him what he wanted.

He smiled his crooked smile. "Well, if that's all you got to worry about, you got it knocked, Miss Hannah. Elizabeth I can't do anything about. But I promise you, you can take me and Petey off the worry list. We're going to watch Kissyfur cartoons, and we're going to check out a few people who might have seen Elizabeth. Okay?"

She stared back at him, drawing comfort from the melancholy calm she saw in his eyes. "Okay," she finally said.

"Damn right. Now—if we can do something about that Perry Mason outfit."

"What is the matter with this outfit!" she cried.

"Well, Hannah, I'll tell you what's the matter . . . You want me to tell you what's the matter?"

"Tell me, tell me."

"Okay. It's like a . . . plain brown wrapper."

"I beg your pardon?" she said.

"You know—some things you can order through the mail and they promise they'll send it to you in a plain brown wrapper—"

"Ernie, what has that got to do with anything!"

"Now, wait. See, when that package in the plain brown wrapper comes, everybody who sees it just *knows* there's something wicked in there, and everybody is busy as hell wondering what it is. Now, you walk into a business meeting dressed like that, and you think you're looking all efficient and everything—well, I'm telling you, Hannah, there won't be a man in the place who's not wondering what's in that plain—"

"I get the picture!" Hannah interrupted, trying not to grin. "You really are . . . full of it, you know that?"

"Yeah, I know that. I just didn't know you did." He was trying to keep a straight face, too, but they both laughed.

"Give 'em hell, Miss Hannah," he told her on her way out, giving her a hard hug as if he knew she needed it, regardless of the suit and the briefcase, and leaving her all addled and ridiculously reassured. She replayed the moment in her mind all day, his warmth and his masculine soap and leather scent, and the strength of his hard male body. For a moment, just a moment, she'd pressed her face into that place at his neck: the place in the V of his undershirt where she could see the beginnings of the curling hair on his chest. It had been entirely pleasant—wonderful—no matter how hard she tried to deny it.

She had to work late, and she looked up just after nine to see Ernie and Petey through the glass windows of the studio, the misery in Petey's face abating somewhat at the sight of Anna-Hannah working hard on her 'mercial just the way she had at home.

"Sorry," Ernie whispered to her when she came out into the hall. "I think she's scared you'll go off, like Libby."

Petey, what are we going to do? Hannah thought as she held out her arms to the child. She stood in the dimly lit hallway, holding a silent Petey tightly and leaning against the wall. Someone opened a door nearby and Hannah could hear the noise of KHRB's eight-o'clock supermovie until the door closed again. She kissed Petey on the cheek and looked up into Ernie's eyes, familiar now with the feelings of helplessness coping with Elizabeth's disappearance generated.

"Hey," he said, reaching to catch a strand of her hair that had come unpinned and place it carefully behind her ear. The light brush of his fingers against her face was like a jolt of lightning. "What you two need is a big brown milk shake."

But there weren't enough big brown milk shakes in the world to assuage Hannah's worry. Petey was becoming more and more attached to her, and Hannah was beginning to look forward to their evenings together, evenings that more often than not included Ernie, with the three of them piling on the living room couch while Hannah told Petey bedtime stories. Petey's favorites—and Ernie's, too, she was beginning to suspect—were about Anna-Hannah's halcyon days as Little Girl Hannah with Grandmama Browne, traveling around the country and living in motor courts or small town hotels or trailer parks with neon names like the Evening Breeze, or the New Alma, or the Blue Bird of Happiness. She told Petey about the things her grandmother had called "life's little surprises"—a carousel in the middle of nowhere, twilight and a wheatfield full of fireflies, a first snow, chocolate cake.

Hannah was only too aware that the ten days were running out. She had tried everyone and everywhere she knew to try to locate Elizabeth, and she couldn't expect Ernie to hang around forever—as much as she might want it. She tried telling herself that it was just that she was . . . comfortable having him around, even though he drove her crazy with his personal questions and his more personal looks. And his damn personal telephone calls—ones that came in night and day on *her* telephone as the news spread among the honky-tonk angels of Dallas–Fort Worth that John Ernest Watson was back in town. He never seemed to *do* anything about the women who called, but to Hannah, the Marlenes and Selenas and the Modestas who telephoned all the time were just one more reason why she shouldn't look forward to seeing him the way she did, or to having him stay for dinner, or to being able to talk to him.

"What did you do?" Hannah said testily. "Post my number in the ladies' room of every cowboy dive between here and Amarillo? It's supposed to be unlisted, you know!"

Ernie grinned and took his own good time about answering. "Yeah, Hannah," he said, "I did. All the places where Libby goes."

"He's just a warm, friendly person, that's all," Hannah whispered to herself in the kitchen one evening because she was worn out with trying to ignore him, and that was the safest reason she could think of to explain her growing infatuation. She couldn't keep from looking at him, damn it all, and he seemed always to be expecting her to do just that. She realized he must think she had some kind of crush on him—like all the women who telephoned him, there was no way for him *not* to think it.

On the weekend, he insisted on taking her and Petey to Fort Worth for the start of the Cowtown rodeo season. He took them behind the chutes to what initially reminded Hannah of some kind of macho western ballet class. It was smelly with manure and animals, dirt and popcorn. It was dusty, littered with Styrofoam cups, cigarette butts, and army surplus duffel bags. And it was crowded with cowboy athletes who warmed up and stretched out while they talked bulls, broncs, and women—in that order—and spat tobacco juice. Through it all, the clang of the chute gates and the blare of the rodeo announcer and the cheers of the enthusiastic crowd sounded.

It was obvious to Hannah that Ernie Watson was in some kind of heaven, so much so that she couldn't keep from smiling. He was definitely one of the boys. Every cowboy who wasn't in the arena must have come up to shake his hand.

"You working tonight, Ernie?" a particularly young cowboy wearing turquoise leather chaps wanted to know.

"Not tonight, kid."

"Aw, hell," he said as if he meant it, shooting a look of apology at Hannah. "I don't trust nobody but you to keep that bull away from my backside. You hear what happened to old Keith in Mesquite?"

Ernie hadn't, and the young cowboy launched into a vivid description of "old Keith's" difficulties. Hannah meant to take Petey and politely move aside so they could have their conversation in private, but Ernie reached out to catch her hand, his rough fingers sliding between hers.

"Don't leave," he said quietly, looking into her eyes. His fingers were warm and strong as they caressed hers, and he kept her close to him while the young cowboy continued to talk. Hannah's knees had gone so weak she couldn't have left even if she'd wanted to. She stood there, aware of nothing but Ernie's warm hand around hers, staring at his profile while he listened intently to some happening with an inexperienced rodeo clown and a particularly rank bull in the Mesquite arena, and hanging on to Petey with her other hand.

This is not going to work, she kept thinking. *This is not going to work . . .*

"What?" Ernie asked when the young man had gone, poking her in the side with his elbow.

She didn't answer, and he let go of her hand, picking up Petey and carrying her to the fence to see the smiling girl on the white horse ride in with the American flag. The house lights dimmed, and the girl's red, white, and blue sequined outfit glittered in the spotlight as her white horse pranced around the arena. Rodeo folk were a patriotic bunch, and the applause was deafening. Hannah felt the familiar lump in her throat as the first strains of the national anthem boomed over the audience. She had been in too many small towns on the Fourth of July, seen too many real celebrations with the home-cooked food and the marching veterans and the late-night fireworks not to get all misty-eyed every time she heard it. She stood in the darkness and wiped furtively at her eyes.

Ernie leaned down, his head close to hers. "You are something else, Miss Hannah," he whispered. "Come on—I promised Petey a face," he said when the lights came back on.

Hannah had no idea what that meant, but she tagged along anyway—to a little corner near a back hallway where a small folding table held a greasepaint kit. He turned over a ten-gallon bucket and made her sit on it with Petey on her lap while he turned Petey into a genuine rodeo clown—and drew a crowd. Nothing would do but that he fix Hannah's face as well, and even in greasepaint, she was having a wonderful time, both because Petey seemed to enjoy herself so and because she hadn't done anything on the spur of the moment in ages —other than assuming responsibility for her wayward sister's child. She firmly suppressed the notion that her good mood had anything to do with Ernie. For about three seconds.

"Now, I tell you," one of the kibitzers said. "I can see why *you* wear that stuff, Ernie—you're just plain damn ugly—but what are you covering up those two pretty faces for?"

Ernie laughed and kept right on drawing freckles on Hannah's cheeks—bigger ones than she and Petey already had.

"And she's got to have a red nose, doesn't she, Petey?" the kibitzer said.

"Yeah!" Petey cried. "A big red nose!"

"So what do you think?" Ernie asked when he'd finished, showing the two of them their faces in a hand mirror.

"Two clowns, Anna-Hannah!" Petey said in delight, marveling at her reflection much the way she did when she put on Hannah's pink satin sleep shirt.

"Smile!" a cowboy called over Ernie's shoulder, catching the moment in a Polaroid snapshot, which he handed to Ernie.

"Let us see," Hannah said, because Ernie was taking such a long time looking at it. It was a good photograph, natural and spontaneous; she and Petey looked more like mother and daughter than aunt and niece. Hannah had every intention of keeping it, but Ernie took it back again, sticking it in his shirt pocket without comment. In fact, it seemed to Hannah that everything he did after that he did without comment. Once, when they were standing at the pens watching the bull-riding and the working clowns, he took her hand again, but he let go abruptly, as if he'd forgotten himself or had breached some personal limit he'd set. He took Petey off to get popcorn, and when he returned, he let her stand down with her popcorn box while he reached into his hip pocket for his handkerchief.

"Here, Hannah, let me get that stuff off your face before they draft you to work the arena," he said, suddenly as bent on getting the clown makeup off her face as he'd been about putting it on.

"Not me," Petey said, pulling on her jeans pocket.

"No, not you, Pete. You keep yours. You're a good sport, Miss Hannah," he said quietly as he scrubbed her face with his handkerchief. She looked up at that comment, trying to meet his eyes. He wouldn't look at her.

Oh, Lord, she thought suddenly. *He's not going to make it through the ten days.*

Petey was sleeping the sweet sleep of exhaustion when they finally arrived home, and Ernie carried her into the bedroom to tuck her in. Hannah busied herself in the kitchen, thinking he'd probably put Petey down and just leave. He hadn't spoken ten words in the last hour, and there was no reason for her to think he'd hang around so he could *not* talk to her.

She was standing at the kitchen sink, washing the few breakfast dishes she hadn't had time to do earlier. She didn't see Ernie until he reached around her and turned off the faucet. He took a cereal bowl out of her hands and set it on the counter, then he reached up, pressing the warm roughness of his palms against the soft skin of her face—a face that still had traces of greasepaint on it.

"What?" she said as his thumb brushed lightly over her lower lip. She tried to look into the eyes moving so intently over her face. Her heart was pounding, and she knew perfectly well *what,* but she said it anyway.

"Hannah, you know what's happening, don't you?" he said in that soft, whispery voice of his. "I'm tired, honey. I'm tired of pretending I don't want to do this—"

With that, he nuzzled her cheek, placing a small kiss just at the corner of her mouth. Another one followed on the bridge of her nose, then her eyebrow, and by the time he reached her mouth again, Hannah considered the possibility of dying from the sheer pleasure of it.

I shouldn't do this, she thought vaguely. But she wasn't doing it; he was. He'd said so . . .

She gave a soft moan and clutched the back of his shirt with her wet hands as his mouth covered hers. He tasted of popcorn, and there was nothing hesitant about him. His approach was uncomplicated and basic. She could feel it in the press of his body against hers, in the quickening of his breath, in the faint tremor of his hands.

I'm a man; you're a woman. I want you.

She broke away from him, pressing her face into his shoulder to savor his heady masculine scent, but he was having none of that. His hands slid into her hair, bringing her around so he could kiss her again. She parted her lips for him because she knew he wanted it. *She* wanted it. She wanted to be explored, tasted, and he was doing just that.

"Ernie," she murmured, making a flagrantly token protest.

"Hush," he whispered, clearly recognizing it for what it was.

She hushed—and offered him her mouth again. He

took it, sweetly, thoroughly. From somewhere far away, it occurred to her that she had never been kissed like this. Or if she had, she hadn't enjoyed it like this, responded like this.

Suddenly he stopped and leaned back to look at her as if he'd just had another one of his horrible thoughts.

"Well, one thing's for damn sure," he announced. "The two of us can't be alone together without getting in trouble." He took her arms from around his neck. "I got to go—"

"Ernie!" Hannah said in exasperation, following him out of the kitchen. "Where are you going?" This man was going to drive her completely up the wall!

"I just got to go—*go!*" he said, waving one hand in the air but not looking at her.

"Why?"

"*Why?*" he said incredulously, as if he had never heard such a stupid question and never hoped to again.

"Yes, *why?*"

He turned around to look at her. "Because!"

"Because why?"

"Because I haven't been with a woman in a long time, and I don't want it to be you, that's why!"

"Well, thanks a lot, Ernie!" she said, marching past him to open the front door. He was still batting a thousand when it came to raising a woman's confidence score.

"Hannah, you know what I mean . . ."

"Yes, I do," she said, holding the door wide. "I'm not Elizabeth. If you're in such a hurry to go—by all means, go!"

He was about to say something, but didn't, looking around him instead.

"What are you looking for!"

"My damn hat!"

Hannah got to it first and threw it at him.

"Hannah?" he said when he reached the door again. "I'm not coming back."

CHAPTER FOUR

HANNAH BELIEVED HIM. There was no doubt in her mind that he meant what he said. But she waited for him anyway, finally giving up when she was nearly an hour late for work. She supposed she should be grateful; at least he hadn't just disappeared. She called the station manager.

"Hannah, I know these are unusual circumstances," he said. "You're doing a wonderful job for us, and we don't want to lose you, but as small as we are—when even one person is out, it really puts us in a bind. You're going to have to get this thing with your niece worked out."

"Yes," she agreed. It was only fair for one's employer to expect one to be able to come to work.

"Today," he added.

Oh, God, Hannah thought as she hung up the phone. She spent the next hour looking through the classified ads and calling day-care centers. Rick had been right; the good ones required immunization records and birth certificates, and the private individuals who looked after children charged prices she couldn't begin to pay. She called friends with children, acquaintances—even near strangers—in the hope of finding *something* for Petey. She had no luck whatsoever.

She closed her eyes for a moment, sitting at the kitchen table with her hands over her face, trying not to give in to her despair. But, it wasn't the lack of baby-sitters that was making her feel so desperate. She was miserable because Ernie had gone, and because he loved Elizabeth.

You knew that! she chided herself. The night they'd met, he'd told her he had once wanted to marry Elizabeth. She could understand why she felt so guilty: She hadn't given her sister a single thought while she'd been in Ernie's arms, and if she'd had any loyalty to Elizabeth, she wouldn't have let herself get so involved in the first place. But why did she feel so rejected? What were a few hot and heavy looks and a little fumbling in the kitchen? Nothing to a man like John Ernest Watson.

And everything to a fool like me . . .

She had to get hold of herself. She had enough problems without indulging in this . . . whatever it was, over Ernie. *Okay, Hannah Rose,* she told herself. *So what? You like him. You like him a lot. You like him more than any man since—*

No! She didn't want to think about that. She was unhappy enough without calling up another major case of rejection. She looked up at a small noise. Petey was standing in the doorway with Cowpoke under her arm, her clown face still in evidence but a bit the worse for wear.

"Where's Ernie?" she asked immediately.

"Petey. Good morning. He . . . can't come. Looks like it's just you and me today. What do you say we wash our face and make something good for breakfast?" She got up from the table, glancing at Petey and knowing instantly that her feeble attempt at cheerfulness hadn't fooled this child for a moment. Petey had spent her life with Elizabeth; she'd learned a long time ago to assess the emotional atmosphere and disregard the words.

"Let's go wash," Hannah said, heading toward the bathroom and holding out her hand.

"No, Anna-Hannah, I'm a clown. Like Ernie. Where's Ernie, Anna-Hannah?"

"I told you, Petey. He can't come today. Let's go wash your face."

"No, no, Anna-Hannah! I'm a clown!"

Hannah hesitated, her mind working furiously to decide how to handle this.

"So you are. I forgot. How about some oatmeal and peaches?" she said after a moment, wondering if she was being reasonable or wishy-washy. She couldn't see any point in forcing Petey to wash the makeup off. Petey had loved having her face painted; it was only natural she'd want to keep it for a while.

She braced herself for more questions about Ernie's whereabouts, but Petey only clutched Cowpoke and watched solemnly as Hannah put together the instant oatmeal and fruit breakfast for her. But, Petey's first tentative spoonful around Cowpoke sent the entire bowl into her lap and then bouncing onto the floor. She looked down at the heap of warm oatmeal on her night-gown, tears welling up in her eyes and her bottom lip trembling.

"Go get Ernie, Anna-Hannah!" she said as the tears began to spill down her face.

"No, it's all right," Hannah said, trying to soothe her. "We can take care of it—"

"No! No! Get Ernie, Anna-Hannah! Get Ernie!"

"Petey!" Hannah said in exasperation. "It's just oatmeal. We can do it. Just let me get your gown off."

"No, Anna-Hannah. I want Ernie! Make him come here!"

"Petey, I don't know where he is," Hannah said, still trying to scoop the oatmeal out of her lap and feeling near tears herself. "Let me have your hand, honey."

But Petey was waving both hands frantically and crying loudly.

"Petey, please—"

"I want Ernie to come here!"

Hannah scraped off as much of the oatmeal as she could and finally picked Petey up and carried her into the bathroom. Inconsolable, she continued to cry, switching her attention suddenly from Ernie to her mother.

"Where's my mommy? Make my mommy come here, Anna-Hannah!"

"Oh, baby," Hannah whispered, hugging her tightly. She had no idea what to say, no words of comfort. She could only stand there with oatmeal and greasepaint all over her and let Petey cry. How could she make a child understand what she didn't understand herself?

"It's all right, Petey," she kept whispering, but they both knew it wasn't true.

The phone rang, and, still carrying Petey, Hannah

went to answer it. She was afraid to let it go because it might be Elizabeth. She tried to put Petey down on the couch—Lord knew, she was little comfort to the child —but Petey clung to her desperately. She answered the telephone with Petey in her arms, still sobbing.

"It's me," the male voice said, and her heart began to pound. Ernie might not come back, but he was keeping his promise to Petey that he'd call. "What's wrong?" he asked.

"Ernie, I can't talk to you now," Hannah said over Petey's crying. As much as she wanted to, needed to, she couldn't. He was the one who had left; she had to remember that.

"What's wrong!"

"I can't talk to you now!"

"Let me talk to Petey, Hannah."

He was still upset; she could hear it in his voice. She closed her eyes and took a deep breath.

"Ernie, I don't think she will," she said, because Petey had finally acknowledged her mother was gone, and Ernie, beloved though he was, as a disembodied voice, wasn't likely to be of much help. "You can try." She held the receiver to Petey's ear, but she only cried louder.

"Hannah, what's wrong with her?"

"Ernie, I can't—she wants her mother. I have to go—"

"Hannah, wait! Are you and Petey all right?"

No. No, we're not all right.

"Yes. You don't have to worry about us. Thank you for calling."

"Hannah, I have to talk to you!"

"Not now, Ernie. Please."

She made herself hang up the phone, swallowing

hard to control the burning ache in her throat. The last thing she needed was to cry, too, and having to face her stupidity about John Ernest Watson was enough to undo the last remnants of her control. She carried Petey back into the bathroom, talking to her continuously, a soft running account of what she was about to do next to get the oatmeal off and leave the face unwashed, but to get the hair brushed and braided. Petey still cried, less hysterically and more desperately, suffering it all in tearful misery.

Damn you, Elizabeth! Hannah thought at one point, because Petey, trembling and afraid, again pleaded, "Make my mommy come here, Anna-Hannah."

Dressing them both in clean jeans and T-shirts, Hannah led Petey back into the living room. She intended to sit down and take her onto her lap, but someone pounded on the front door. Petey's crying immediately intensified, and she clung to Hannah with all the desperation that Hannah herself was feeling.

Hannah answered the door the same way she'd answered the phone—carrying Petey. Strange, she thought, that she couldn't make Petey stop crying, and yet the child still wanted the comfort of her arms.

No one was there. Just a photocopy of the standard apartment lease taped to the door—with the No Children clause circled in black Magic Marker and punctuated with exclamation marks.

"Great!" she said, snatching it off. "Subtle, but to the point." She crumpled it in her hand and slung it toward the nearest wastebasket. It bounced off the rim and landed on the rug. She kicked the door shut, only to have someone knock on it again almost immediately. Expecting the building superintendent, she hugged Petey tightly and gave her a kiss on the cheek, breathing deeply a few times to shore up her courage before she opened it.

Ernie was standing there with his thumbs hooked in his jeans pockets, looking about as haggard as she felt. She had never in her life been bombarded with so many conflicting emotions. She was angry with him for leaving the way he had, and embarrassed that her response to his kiss had precipitated it, and relieved that he'd come back again—all at the same time. She wanted to tell him to go away, and she wanted to fall into his arms. But she stood still and said nothing, looking into his eyes.

Ernie had never been one for waiting to be asked in, and he didn't wait now, stepping inside and attempting to take Petey out of her arms. Still crying, Petey reached for him with one arm and held on to Hannah's neck with the other, locking them into a three-way embrace much the way she had that day under the umbrella.

He took his hat off and gave it a haphazard toss. "Who is this, Miss Hannah?" he said, kissing Petey on the forehead. "Do I know who this is?" After a moment's hesitation, he put his arms around both of them, and Hannah had the distinct feeling he wanted to kiss her on the forehead as well. It was all she could do not to lean into him.

"Me—" Petey said, her voice wavering.

"Me? I don't know any clowns named Me. Now, let me see . . . This is Miss Hannah over here, so this must be—"

"Petey!" she cried, her tears still streaming down her face.

"Petey! It's not!" Ernie said with such incredulity that Hannah almost smiled. *Watch yourself, Hannah,* she thought. He had been back for ten seconds, and she was just as smitten as ever.

"Where is she?" Ernie continued to tease. "I don't see Petey."

"Here, Ernie," Petey insisted.

"Where?"

"Here," she said, patting herself on the chest.

"Well, dang if it's not. Anna-Hannah, I thought you'd brought the wrong clown home. Here, let old Ernie take you."

This time she let go of Hannah's neck. Ernie stood with her for a moment, patting her on the back, then walked toward the couch to sit down. He still limped, and he still presumed, taking Hannah by the arm and pulling her along with them.

"You through crying, Pete?" he asked, repeating the question he'd asked that first night and painfully lowering his tall frame onto the couch. He glanced at Hannah, and she sat down beside him, trying unsuccessfully to read his look.

Petey shook her head no and continued to cry.

"Well, let me know when, because I want to tell you something. I want to tell you what I think about your mama."

Hannah was about to protest, but he shot her another look. *Trust me.* She pressed her lips together and waited. She could do that easily enough—God help her. Ernie sat with Petey on his lap until she grew quiet.

"This is what I think, Pete," he said when she was calm enough to listen. "Your mama left you with me, and she told me to take you to Anna-Hannah because she had important things to do. And what I think is as soon as she gets through doing those things, she'll be right back to get you. Now, she knows I love you and

Anna-Hannah loves you, so she doesn't have to worry. You don't have to worry either, Pete."

"I want her to hurry," Petey said, her eyes filling with tears again.

"I know you do, Pete. And I've told everybody I know, and Anna-Hannah's told everybody she knows: 'If you see Petey's mama, tell her to *hurry*.' Okay?"

After a very long moment, Petey nodded.

"Now give me a hug," Ernie said to her. "I need one pretty bad today. How about you?"

"Yes," Petey said, her voice still tearful.

"Right," Ernie said, giving her a hug that was more sound effect than squeezing. "Now have you got one for me?"

"And Anna-Hannah, too," Petey decided. "Everybody needs a hug." She gave Ernie his return hug, hugged Hannah and finally slid down from Ernie's lap to find Cowpoke and bring him in to watch television. Hannah got up to go into the kitchen, exhausted from the emotional trials of the morning and needing some kind of busywork to keep her mind off the man who was openly watching her every move. She just didn't know what he wanted from her! She hadn't from the first night he limped into her life. He liked her, she thought, but he certainly didn't want to. She had sensed the struggle he was having with himself all along, and she couldn't attribute it to anything but his regard for Elizabeth. The fact that a man was in love with one woman didn't necessarily keep him from being attracted to another. It was his sense of honor and decency that kept him from doing anything about it, and John Ernest Watson, if last night was any example, was a decent, honorable man.

She began cleaning up the rest of the spilled oatmeal,

wiping up places she'd already wiped because Ernie had followed her to the kitchen.

"She hasn't had any breakfast," she said after a time. She wanted to tell him how good she thought he was with Petey, but she didn't want him to think she was trying to compromise him—again.

"I think she'll be asleep in a minute. She's pretty worn out," he answered, his eyes trying to hold hers. "What happened?"

"She . . . spilled her oatmeal." Hannah looked away and kept wiping the table. "It was all downhill from there."

"I should have told her I was leaving. What did you tell her?"

"I told her the truth. I told her you wouldn't be here today and that I didn't know where you were."

"I was standing by a damn pay telephone trying not to call you, that's where I was," he said testily.

"Look! You didn't have to come back here. We would have been all right—and what are you mad at *me* for? *I* haven't done anything!"

"Oh, no? You've just upset my whole damn life, that's all!"

"I beg your pardon!" Hannah said indignantly.

"You heard me! But neither one of us has got the time to worry about that now. I called my aunt Mim in Tahlequah right after I talked to you. She wants you to bring Petey to her as soon as you can. Today—"

"I can't do that," Hannah interrupted. "I have to work, and Lord knows we don't want *me* to upset *your* life anymore."

"You have to take her," he said stubbornly. "Mim's heard from Libby."

CHAPTER FIVE

"WHERE IS SHE?"

"Mim doesn't know."

"She doesn't *know!* Then why am I supposed to take Petey to her?" Hannah said, whispering so that Petey wouldn't hear them. But the trouble with whispering was that Ernie had to come closer to hear her.

Maybe he really had been standing by a pay telephone, she thought as she looked up at him. He looked so tired. She could see the fatigue in his eyes, and she suppressed the urge to touch him, trying hard not to look away. The morning had been awful, and the rest of the day was showing no signs of improvement. Lord, she wanted him to put his arms around her!

"This is Libby we're talking about here, Hannah, not

a Greyhound bus. She wouldn't keep a schedule—even if she did happen to make one. All she told Mim was that she'd be there sometime tomorrow. With Libby, that could mean any time—night or day."

"What did Elizabeth say about Petey?"

"Nothing."

"Nothing! I'm supposed to take Petey there when Elizabeth obviously still doesn't want her?"

"Hannah, look. Neither one of us knows what's going on, and we're not about to find out until we talk to Libby. You don't have anybody to leave Petey with, so we're going to have to take her along."

"We?"

"Yes, *we*. You and me."

"You're not coming with me," Hannah said stubbornly. And she meant it. How could she go to Oklahoma with him and not make a bigger fool of herself than she already had? And what was the matter with him anyway? They couldn't be together and not get into trouble—*his* words.

"Have you ever been to Tahlequah?"

"No, but I can read a map like nobody's business. I had to all those years I traveled around with my mother."

"Maybe so. But you don't know all the shortcuts I know. We want to get there ahead of Libby, in case she won't wait. Now, you know she's as apt to go as she is to stay and wait for us, Petey or no Petey."

Hannah pulled out a chair and sat down at the kitchen table. She had no argument for that. None. She took a deep breath and tried to think.

"Hannah, I want to go with you. I don't want to worry about you and Petey on the road alone when you don't know where you're going."

She looked up at him, losing herself for a moment in his sad, dark eyes. If he'd put it any other way—made it a demand instead of a statement of fact—she would have dug her heels in. Damn it all, she cared about him. She didn't want to worry him. She didn't want his life to be turned upside down, even if he did insist she was the cause of it. In her opinion, it was six of one and half a dozen of the other as to just whose life had been upset by whom. "All right," she said, because she needed him and she needed to give in to his logic. She tried not to think that the real reason he wanted to go had to be Elizabeth.

He looked so relieved that she nearly put her hand out to touch him, after all.

"Do you chew tobacco?" she asked abruptly instead, and he grinned.

"Hannah, you've been with me night and day for almost ten days. Have you seen me chew?"

"Answer the question!"

"What for!"

"Because I'm not traveling anywhere with somebody who's going to be spitting tobacco juice!"

"I tell you one thing, Hannah, between my dumb reasons and your dumb questions, it's a wonder either one of us gets let out by ourselves."

"Do you or don't you?"

"Not when I'm sober! I have to be drunk to stand the taste of it. All right?"

"All right!"

"All right!" he repeated.

"Just so you know," she said to underscore her position.

"Just so I know?" he said incredulously. "You give

me hell about not chewing tobacco when I don't chew, and I'm supposed to *know?*"

"It makes as much sense as anything else that's happened around here lately," she said significantly.

"Well, now, you got me there, Hannah. You going to work?"

"No, I'm not going to work. Petey's had enough of musical caretakers for one day."

The remark was unfair, and she knew it. Petey wasn't his responsibility, even if he had been willing to stay in Dallas and help take care of her until last night. Ernie made no comment, though it was plain enough by the way he pressed his lips together that he wanted to.

"How soon can you be ready?" he said after a long pause.

"I have to stop at the station before I go."

"We can do that on the way. I'll be back in about an hour," he said, and he left her alone in the kitchen, still wiping up imaginary oatmeal.

Petey had fallen asleep. Hannah used the time to pack a few things for this mad trip to Oklahoma, making a great effort not to concern herself about Ernie's whereabouts—not an easy thing to do when he had two telephone calls from the same strange-voiced female while he was gone, one who wouldn't leave a message. It was early afternoon and raining when he returned. He'd changed his clothes, and he'd had a haircut, of all things. He was still wearing his cowboy garb—jeans and a plaid shirt and a denim jacket. But he looked so *groomed* somehow. And masculine. And handsome. Hannah didn't comment, but she couldn't keep her eyes off him, and he kept catching her at it.

"Fifteen bucks!" he finally snapped, snatching off his hat and pointing to his freshly barbered hair. "Okay?"

"And worth every penny," she assured him, whether she should have or not. "You're gorgeous."

He grinned, a little embarrassed, a little shy, and clearly pleased.

"Elizabeth will love it," she added, and his grin faded.

Petey let her face be washed, and Hannah told Ernie about his telephone calls. He made no comment, and they were ready to leave by two. It was still raining. Ernie and Petey waited in Ernie's beat-up, no-color pickup truck in the KHRB parking lot while she went inside. She dreaded having to see the station manager, dreaded having to ask him for more time off, but there was no help for it. She fully expected to come out of his office unemployed.

"What happened?" Ernie asked the minute she returned, hardly giving her time to get in out of the rain and close the truck door.

"What happened?" Petey echoed, and Hannah smiled, letting out the breath she'd been holding practically from the time she'd gone in.

"He let me have the rest of the week—until next Monday. He's even going to take over my reading class," she said, still in a daze. "Those two furniture outlet scripts I just did—the man bought them." She looked at Ernie and grinned. "Lord, I feel like the weight of the world's been lifted—till next Monday, anyway."

"You look like it, too. Nice to see that smile again." He stared into her eyes until they both grew awkward, then started the truck and headed for Garland and Route 75 north. He'd insisted on driving, recuperating knee or not, and Hannah settled back, her mind wandering as she half-listened to Petey happily chattering to Cowpoke and the rhythmic, hypnotic sound of the windshield wipers. Her spirits rose, in spite of the weather and the reason for the trip, and in spite of a sudden attack of nostalgia. When her mother was alive, a spur-of-the-moment excursion like this had been one of her favorite things, and she'd continued her travels long after other women her age had settled down in a rocking chair by a quiet hearth.

"What are you thinking about?" Ernie said, breaking into her reverie.

"Oh—Little Girl Hannah, I guess. And Grandmama Browne. She loved a trip like this. She liked to just hop in the car and go. When I was ten, we were living in Greenville, South Carolina. I came home from school one Friday, and she said, 'Have you ever seen the mighty Mississippi, Hannah Rose?' She knew perfectly well I hadn't or, if I had, I didn't remember it. The next thing I knew, I was in a blue and white 'fifty-three Chevrolet Bel Air coupe with a toothbrush and a change of underwear, and heading west. She liked to stop at these little community stores in the middle of nowhere —those places where they slice up their own meat and cheese. She'd buy a loaf a bread and a half-pound of bologna, and we'd pull off the road someplace and make sandwiches. It was wonderful. She worked as a waitress most of the time—really long hours. She couldn't be a grade mother or a den mother, but she drove a whole weekend just so I could spit in the Mississippi River." She glanced at Ernie, then let her eyes linger because at that moment he was watching the road.

I love to look at him, she thought crazily, the thought presenting itself even though she knew perfectly well she couldn't afford to indulge in that kind of wistfulness.

He glanced at her. "Tell me something."

"What?"

"Have you seen Rick what's-his-name since Petey's been staying with you?"

"Archer," she supplied, wondering where that question came from. "No. Why?"

"Talked to him?"

"No. Why?" she said again.

"I was just wondering."

They were on the road nearly an hour before he asked what was really on his mind, driving in a heavy downpour on the nearly desolate stretch of road outside Sherman.

"Hannah, how . . . involved were you with Archer?"

"None of your business," Hannah said quietly, because it wasn't and because she didn't want to answer him.

He was about to say something else, but she looked at him hard over Petey's head.

"Okay, fine," he said a little shortly. "Then you can tell me why you didn't get married to that guy you were supposed to marry—the one *before* Rick what's-his-name. Libby told me one time her baby sister was getting married. Why didn't you?"

"Don't you think you're getting a little personal here?"

"You ain't seen nothing yet, Hannah Rose," he advised her, looking at her long enough to make her worry about his driving. "And I told you before: I don't waste time working up to something."

"Will you look where you're going!"

"I am looking where I'm going. Why didn't you

marry him? You find out you didn't care anything about him or what?"

She didn't answer him.

"What was his name—Williamson?"

She looked at him for a long moment. Elizabeth had told him more about her than he'd ever said. "Yes," she said finally. "Williamson. Nathan Williamson."

"Libby said he broke your heart. Did he?"

"Yes, Ernie, he broke my heart. We wanted different things. I had a career. He wanted a housewife. I loved him; he loved me, but somehow we missed knowing that about each other until it was nearly time for the wedding. He couldn't believe I wouldn't give up my job and be just Mrs. Williamson, the mother of his children. I couldn't believe he'd ask me to do it. I thought we could work it out—compromise. I thought that right up until the time he married somebody else. Okay?"

"That's why you got so caught up in your job at the big station downtown," he said perceptively.

"That's why," she agreed. "It was the least I could do, considering my degree of sacrifice and personal pain."

"And you regret it?"

She thought before she answered. "No. There were other differences, things I thought wouldn't matter then, but they probably would have eventually."

"What things?"

"Ernie—"

"Hannah, I want to know. Tell me."

"He grew up in a stable traditional family. I didn't. And I don't think he would have ever let me just up and throw the kids in the car and drive them to the Mississippi River so they could spit in it."

"No?" he asked, grinning.

"No," she assured him.

"Hannah, about last night," he said abruptly. "It didn't come out the way I meant. I said it all wrong—"

"I don't want to talk about that, Ernie. I mean it."

"Hannah—"

"Ernie, it doesn't matter! Elizabeth is my sister. I love her." *We both do,* she thought. She was afraid he was going to insist, but he didn't, probably because Petey chose that moment to interrupt her chat with Cowpoke and look up at them. The conversation turned to lighter things, to more about Little Girl Hannah and to how long it would be until they could stop for a brown milk shake. Hannah could feel that Ernie was only postponing his explanation of his abrupt departure last night. One of life's little quirks, she thought resignedly. When they'd first met, she'd given him the chance to tell her about his commitment to Elizabeth. He hadn't taken it, and now, when she didn't want to hear it, he was going to insist on telling her.

They stopped along the road for something to eat, Petey and Hannah waiting in the truck while Ernie dashed inside a place with a flat roof and chipping paint and a neon name, Starlight Café, in the big front window. He was a regular; she could tell by the big hug he got from the woman in pink hair curlers at the cash register. He brought the woman closer to the window and pointed at his pickup truck. The woman smiled and waved, and Hannah and Petey dutifully returned the silent greeting. And the Starlight Café—as Ernie had promised—served excellent hamburgers and brown milk shakes. The cab of the truck was filled with the wonderful aroma of toasted bread and onion-flavored meat.

"Come here often, do you?" Hannah asked, because

the entire staff was now in the window waving as they pulled away.

He grinned. "I'd take you inside if we had the time. That's Ozelle—the one with the curlers. The woman's crazy about me."

Hannah grinned in return, relaxing a bit in the truce they were enjoying. She had no idea where they were—somewhere between McAlester and Muskogee to the best of her calculations. They'd passed all those bodies of water—or perhaps it was one large and irregular body of water. She really couldn't tell in the rain with the daylight nearly gone. Petey remained chipper and wide awake, much to Hannah's relief. As long as she was awake, Ernie wasn't likely to insist they talk about last night.

It was dark by the time they neared Muskogee, and Ernie pulled off on the side of the road.

"How about driving for a while, Hannah. My knee's killing me."

She gave him a worried look, one he couldn't see in the darkness of the cab. He got out and limped around to the other side while she climbed over Petey.

"Are you . . . okay?" she asked as he got in on the passenger side, the worry he couldn't see now perfectly audible in her voice.

"Yeah, I'm okay. It just hurts. I got the clamps out today. We've got about thirty more miles. Just go into Muskogee on 69 here, and come out of it on Route 62."

That seemed to be the extent of his directions, because he pulled his hat down over his eyes and slid down in the seat.

"Are you sleepy, Ernie?" Petey wanted to know—a very timely question in Hannah's opinion. He was supposed to show her shortcuts, not sleep. He certainly seemed to put a lot of stock in her claim she could read a map—if she had a map.

"Yeah, Pete. I am," he said, looking out from under his hat.

"I'm not," she assured him.

He laughed. "Yeah, and green vegetables look like marshmallows. How about leaning back here and singing me a song. Sing 'Honky Tonk Man.'"

Petey sang with great enthusiasm, and Ernie again disappeared under his hat. Hannah drove carefully into the rainy night, following Route 69 the way he'd told her, and both he and Petey were fast asleep before they reached Muskogee. She found Route 62 to Fort Gibson with minimal bother, and she didn't wake him until they were a few miles out of Tahlequah.

"What?" he murmured at the pressure of her hand on his arm.

"We're almost in Tahlequah," she said.

He sat up and looked around. "Are we? Okay— drive straight through town. On the road going out, look for a mailbox with the name Swimmer. Less than a mile out, on the right."

"Swimmer," she repeated.

"Right. Have you ever been in Oklahoma before?"

"Not awake," she said, switching the heater to defrost to clear the fogged-up windshield.

"So what do you think of it?"

"Well, I think it's dark and wet. And flat."

She could feel him grin, and she turned her head to look at him.

"Look where you're going, Hannah," he chided her, and none too soon. She drove intently now, not wanting to get them lost when they were so close to their destination. She could feel Ernie's eyes on her, feel exactly how far away he was from her in the darkness of the truck's cabin. Petey slept sprawled between them, and Ernie swung his arm across the back of the seat. His fingers were only inches from her shoulder. She could feel them so acutely that she drove past the Swimmer mailbox and had to back up on the dark road to make the turn.

Ernie said nothing as she turned into the long, muddy drive that led to the house. She could make out very little—the lights of the house in a grove of trees in the distance. And she was suddenly apprehensive—which was ridiculous. Either her troubles with Elizabeth were about to end, or they weren't, and there was no use fretting about it.

"Park over there," Ernie said, pointing out a spot in the side yard.

Hannah parked the truck, but she sat gripping the steering wheel after she'd turned the engine off, peering out the rain-splattered windshield for who-knew-what in the darkness. The house was small and symmetrical, with a centered front porch and a swing that had been raised high to protect it from the coming winter weather. Leaves from the surrounding trees fell with the rain, sticking to the wet windshield.

"Elizabeth's car isn't here, is it?" she asked as he opened the truck door. She moved Cowpoke aside so he could pick up the still sleeping Petey.

"No," he answered, covering Petey with her yellow poncho. "Hannah?" he said just as he was about to get out into the rain. "I think I'm in love with you."

CHAPTER SIX

"YOU WHAT?"

"You heard me," he said over his shoulder, and he kept going, leaving her sitting there alone.

She scrambled out of the truck, trotting along after him in the rain. "Ernie—"

"Not now, Hannah."

Not now? she thought incredulously. *He casually throws out a statement like that then says,* "Not now?"

He slowed down enough for her to catch up with him, but as she walked along beside him, he deliberately bumped her with his shoulder, making her falter, then grinned from ear to ear because she was ready to punch him in the nose for it. "I just thought you ought to know."

He just thought she out to *know?*

"In case I get busy and I don't get to tell you," he added over his shoulder because Hannah was lagging behind again. "And quit looking like Bambi," he said as he stepped up on the front porch.

"I feel like Bambi," she said.

"Come on, Hannah," he prodded her, because she'd stopped walking and was standing in the rain. She looked up at him with a start and followed him onto the porch. He *thought* he was in love with her. What was that supposed to mean? Besides the fact that he'd just made a difficult situation impossible?

She was about to ask him, but the front door opened and Ernie caught her by the hand.

"Hey, Mim," he said to the woman who opened the door. "Look what I brought you."

"Elizabeth?" Mim said expectantly, flinging the door open wide. "Elizabeth?"

"No," Hannah said. She stood awkwardly for a moment and then extended her hand. "It's Hannah—Elizabeth's sister."

"Hannah," Mim said. "I thought maybe—" Disappointment filled her voice, but she squeezed Hannah's hand warmly. She was a petite woman, a bit plump, with salt-and-pepper hair that hung down her back in a long braid. She was wearing a white dress and a blue checked gingham apron with the bib and pockets decorated in intricate cross-stitching. Hannah remembered Elizabeth's assessment of Mim Swimmer: "She's like Mammy in *Gone with the Wind*." Hannah had no doubt it was true. Mim had taken upon herself the hopeless task of trying to instill a sense of responsibility in Elizabeth Browne, yet her devotion knew no bounds, nor did her forgiveness. She had paid off Elizabeth's traffic tickets to keep the family from knowing about them, hidden her from irate husbands and lovers, held her hand through three divorces and the birth of a child. And she quite obviously still loved her unconditionally.

Now she looked at Hannah closely, then abruptly hugged her and kissed her cheek. A bit bewildered, Hannah could only hug her in return, her mind identifying Mim's pleasant scent as one she had always associated with her mother: Camay soap and Cashmere Bouquet bath powder.

"Come inside," Mim said. "Come in out of the rain. You don't remember me at all, do you?"

"No. I'm sorry," Hannah said truthfully. "I wish I did."

"Ah, well. You were hardly more than a baby the last time I saw you. Nearly two. You've grown into a beautiful woman. Isn't she beautiful, John Ernest? Such beautiful gray-green eyes—"

"Yeah, she's beautiful," Ernie said quietly. "Inside and out."

Hannah glanced at him, thinking that it was kind of him to be so uncharacteristically tactful in the face of a head-to-head comparison between her and Elizabeth, but he wouldn't meet her eyes.

"Let me see your other treasure," Mim said, lifting the yellow poncho off Petey. Petey was awake and waiting.

"Boo!" she said as the poncho came off. "I can't find my mommy," she told Mim immediately. "I can't find her, and Ernie can't find her, and Anna-Hannah can't find her." It was more a statement of fact than a prelude to more emotional distress—Petey's news report for Mim on the current status of things, Hannah thought.

"Can I see my mommy now?"

Mim faltered only for a moment. "The picture book, you mean?" She held out her arms for Petey to come to her. "I have an album of pictures—Petey's mother when she was a little girl," Mim said to Hannah.

"My mommy stayed here and stayed here when she was four," Petey said.

"That's right," Mim told her. "And she always liked to look at my picture book, too. You come with us, Hannah. I have some pictures of you."

"Let me take your jacket, Hannah," Ernie said, his hands warm on her shoulders as he helped her off with her wet jacket, the one she'd worn when she stood in the rain and announced the weather conditions for the big station downtown. He smiled into her eyes for a moment, then left her to follow Mim into the living room. Her mind was still in a turmoil from his startling announcement, and she stared after him as he limped into the kitchen. She gave a soft sigh and turned to find Mim quietly watching, her expression unreadable.

"This way," she said. "Hannah, if you'd bring me the album on the rocking chair."

The room was lamplit, warm, and pleasant, with more evidence of what must be Mim's hobby—cross-stitching—on the throw pillows on the couch and rocking chair and in wooden frames hung on the walls. Hannah didn't want to look at photographs; she wanted to know about Elizabeth, but they were all forced into this conspiracy of silence for Petey's sake. Hannah brought the album, thinking Mim must have been looking at it before they arrived.

She and Petey sat down on the couch with Mim between them. The album was worn, its cover tooled leather with the name *Goingback Swimmer* printed in gold in the lower right-hand corner.

"Goingback was my grandmother's name and mine," Mim said, running her fingertips over the letters. "It comes from the Trail of Tears, from the longing of the Cherokee to go back to their home in the eastern mountains after the Removals to Oklahoma." She suddenly smiled. "When John Ernest was a little boy, Goingback Swimmer was too much for him. Mim, he called me, and Mim I've stayed."

Hannah smiled, thinking of Ernie as a child. She could see into the kitchen from where she sat, see him standing quietly, looking in her direction. He moved out of the doorway, and Mim opened the album. It was filled with pictures of Elizabeth, pictures of her as a toddler, as a sweetheart of the rodeo, as a prom queen. Petey was clearly fascinated—as was Hannah, if the truth be told. It was strange, seeing all these photographs of Elizabeth's life unfolding, a life Hannah would have shared if circumstances had been different. She looked at the pictures closely, trying to imagine herself in them and two years younger than the Elizabeth who was captured there. She couldn't do it.

There was a picture of her mother on a day when she was young and smiling and holding two little girls by the hand.

"Is that Elizabeth and me?" Hannah said incredulously.

"Yes, that's you there—the little one," Mim said. "And here's your father."

She looked at the young man in a suit and tie. He was standing with one foot on a car's running board, and he was just that—a young man. She hadn't known him then, and she didn't know him now.

"Ernie!" Petey declared, tapping a picture with her fingers.

It *was* him. The picture had been taken recently, and he was with Elizabeth. He was sitting on the tailgate of his no-color pickup truck, his arms wrapped around her. They were both laughing, and Hannah felt as if her heart had been ripped out. There could be no future for her and John Ernest Watson, regardless of his qualified declaration of love. One had only to look at this photograph to know it.

"Mim, I need you a minute," Ernie said from the doorway.

"Can't you find the cake?" she asked.

"You got cake?" he asked in mock surprise.

"You know I do, you rascal," she said as she got up from the couch. "I knew you were coming, didn't I? Just keep looking at the pictures," she said to Hannah and Petey. "I'll be right back. I see you got a haircut, John Ernest."

"I had to. You'd give me hell if I didn't."

"John Ernest, I've told you ever since you were a little boy—"

"Yeah, I know, Mim. Get my hair cut and act like I'm *somebody*."

"And don't swear—"

They laughed together, and their conversation became muted as soon as they were out of the room. She could see them both just inside the kitchen doorway, and she knew that Ernie was asking about Elizabeth. As she kept Petey occupied with the photo album, she also knew that whatever Mim told him wasn't good news. His face was grim as he walked back in her direction.

"Cake's ready," he said in the doorway.

I wish I didn't like him, she thought. *If I didn't like him so much, I could handle it.* But she did like him. She liked his honesty about his problem with alcohol.

She liked the way he cared about Petey. She liked the way the other men at the rodeo seemed to respect him —the man first, and his skill as a rodeo clown second. She liked the way he looked and the way he tasted and the way he felt when she had her arms around him. Maybe she even *thought* she was in love with him.

"You better hurry, Pete," he said to the little girl who was already off the couch like a shot. "It's your favorite kind."

"What kind is that?" Hannah asked.

"Brown!" Ernie and Petey said together, and Hannah laughed.

Petey ran on ahead, and Hannah lingered with Ernie for a moment.

"What did Mim say about Elizabeth?"

"Let's get Petey situated," he said, reaching up to briefly brush her cheek with his rough fingers. Hannah felt his touch so intensely that she had to close her eyes. "Then we'll talk."

"Ernie—"

"Come on," he insisted, leading the way to the kitchen.

They ate the chocolate cake at the kitchen table.

"Where's Uncle Michael?" Ernie asked as he handed the plates of cake around.

"Looking," Mim said obscurely, and he didn't ask her to elaborate. It seemed that there was no topic of conversation available to them that didn't sooner or later involve Elizabeth.

"It's raining, Petey," Mim said. "Do you know what that means?"

"No," Petey said, but the tone of Mim's voice obviously had her intrigued.

"Somebody told me you like to dress up," she said,

winking at Ernie. "I've got something new for rainy days: the dress-up box. When you finish your cake, we'll go find it."

The box, which Mim kept in a hall closet, was filled with old clothes and hats, purses and scarves and high-heeled shoes. Petey was in absolute heaven.

"Let's go," Ernie whispered in Hannah's ear.

"Where?"

"You're going to spend the night at my dad's house in case Libby comes there first. I want to take you on over there."

"Why would she do that?"

"Dad doesn't stay in Oklahoma much. Right now he's gone to see one of his old *compañeros* in New Mexico. Mim keeps the house ready for him in case he decides to wander back this way, and she uses it to catch any of the Swimmers' visiting overflow. Libby knows that. If she wants to be by herself, she might go there first and come here later."

"Or if she's looking for you," Hannah said quietly, looking directly into his eyes. He didn't have to leave out things on her account whether he "thought" he was in love with her or not. "What about Petey?" she asked.

"She always stays here with Mim. She's got her own bed."

"I don't want to go off and leave her, Ernie."

"Honey, she's having a ball. Look at her."

That was true enough, Hannah thought, watching Petey try to find the right hat. She picked one with a wide brim and artificial pink roses.

"She's having a ball *now,*" Hannah said, wary of doing anything to make Petey feel any more abandoned than she already did.

"Well, we'll just ask her. Hey, Pete," he called. "I'm

going to take Anna-Hannah over to the old house. You want to go along, or you want to stay here and play?"

"Stay here!" she said, dragging out more clothes.

"See?" Ernie said.

"You really know how to phrase a question, don't you?"

"Hannah, Mim will call you if Petey needs you—but I think she'll be all right here."

Hannah looked at Petey again and gave a tired sigh. "So do I. Let's go."

Ernie went to get her jacket, while she intruded on the fashion show long enough to kiss Petey good-bye.

"Hannah," Mim said quietly while Ernie was gone. "I want to talk to you later. About John Ernest."

Hannah fully intended to tell her there was nothing to talk about, but Ernie came back with a long raincoat-poncho-looking thing that must have come in handy for riding horses in a storm, and she walked with him out onto the porch.

"I'll get your things out of the truck," he said as he put the raincoat on, heading off the question she was about to ask about Elizabeth. "We're going to walk over to my dad's place—yeah, I know it's raining," he added, "but it's shorter if we walk, and I want to show you something."

Petey had moved up from the grocery bag to a nylon duffel bag Hannah had given her, and he brought that as well. She waited on the porch while he took it inside. He had a flashlight with him when he came back out and a somewhat beaten-up cowboy hat, which he plopped on her head without ceremony.

"Let's go."

"What did Mim say?" she asked again as she fell into step with him. The hat kept the rain off her, but it was too big. She had to keep pushing it up to see the wet ground in the beam from the flashlight as they crossed the backyard.

"Libby called to say she wasn't coming."

Hannah stopped walking. "That's crazy. She wouldn't call to say she *wasn't* coming. She just wouldn't come."

"Well, she did. The trick is knowing whether or not she means it. Come on, Hannah, you're getting wet. Hey," he said offhandedly when she caught up with him. "You want to come in here with me?" He held the raincoat wide for her, but she hesitated, clutching her own duffel bag to her chest. She had always traveled light, and it wasn't much to hide behind. And she had a thousand reasons why she shouldn't go to him and only one why she should: She wanted to.

"Come here, Hannah."

Oh, that soft, soft voice . . .

She went, letting him put his arm around her and cover her with half the raincoat. He held her against him for a moment, and she nearly lost her hat. She completely lost her composure. When he started walking again, she went with him, faltering after a few steps.

"It's going to be okay, Hannah."

"No, I don't think so," she answered, knowing he meant one thing, Elizabeth's disappearance, and she meant another, him. They walked on in silence. She could feel the warm pressure of his body along hers, and she felt like crying. How had she gotten into this craziness? He'd spent most of his life taking care of Elizabeth, and even if he hadn't, he was an itinerant with a drinking problem. He never stayed in one place very long. A woman would have to be out of her mind to get involved with him even if she weren't Elizabeth's sister, but there Hannah was stumbling around in the rain and the dark with him, perfectly willing to follow him wherever he wanted to go. .

"Ernie—"

"Wait," he said, holding up his hand. He stopped walking. "I want you to hear something."

"What?"

"Shhh. Listen . . ."

She listened. And heard nothing but the rain.

"I don't—" She stopped. She did hear something: a dull, melodic sound off to her right. "What is that?"

"What do you think it is?" he countered.

"I don't know . . . *Swan Lake?*" she said incredulously. "I hear *Swan Lake!*"

Ernie laughed his endearing soft chuckle. "You want to see? Come on. I want you to see it."

"What is it?" she asked again, clutching the back of his denim jacket under the raincoat as he abruptly changed directions. She had to take big steps to keep up with him, and at one point he hiked her up on his hip so she wouldn't have to wade through a puddle along the way.

"It's some of my dad's craziness—a musical water-wheel. He made it for my mother right before she died. Man, she loved that thing. I mean, who expects to hear the opening bars of *Swan Lake* out here?"

Who indeed? Hannah thought, smiling to herself as she walked along with him. He stopped when they reached a small pond.

"Look over there," he said, shining the flashlight at a small damlike construction at one end. "See, the water turns this drum with pegs in it, and the pegs hit these wooden mallets and make them strike some wine bottles. The bottles have got water in them to give them different pitches—what do you think?"

"I think it's wonderful."

"Yeah, it is," he agreed. "My old man hasn't been able to stay around here very long at a time ever since my mother died. That's why he moved us to New Mexico when I was a kid. But when he comes back, he always fixes the wheel. One time he said he thinks maybe she comes here sometimes, and he wants her to be able to hear it. I guess that sounds a little crazy," he added, looking down at her.

"No," Hannah said. It didn't sound crazy at all. "It sounds like he loved her."

His arm tightened around her. "Yeah. That's one thing they can say about my old man. He loved Kit Crowe."

"What was he like, your father?" Hannah asked impulsively. She had always had a certain curiosity about fathers—probably because she hadn't known her own.

"Oh, he was a loner. Didn't need anybody or anything, he told me, until my mother got ahold of him. He said he didn't know what loneliness meant, didn't know he was drowning in it until he met her. He said she bound him to her with chains as light as gossamer, and he would have died rather than break a single one. Can you imagine a rough old cowboy saying something like 'light as gossamer'?"

"It's . . . nice that you and your dad can talk to each other like that."

"Well, it only took us twenty years or so to get to that point. We didn't talk much at all for a long time. I blamed him for my mother's dying. Not for any reason; he was just handy. I told you I was glad to get to New Mexico, but I wasn't. I blamed him for taking me off when I wanted to stay here with Libby. I was a handful when we got to Chimayo. I didn't want to be there, and I took it out on everybody." He suddenly laughed. "I got my butt kicked for it, too. One of the local boys, Mac McDade, performed what you might call an attitude adjustment on me out behind the corrals one Saturday morning. We've been friends ever since."

"You're a godparent for his children," Hannah remembered, shivering a bit.

"Right. You're cold. Let's go, Miss Hannah. I ought to have more sense than to keep you out here in the rain while I run on about nothing."

But it wasn't just from the cold that she shivered. It was from being close to him and from caring about him and from having him make that crazy announcement they were both now avoiding.

"Which way?" she said, trying to put all that aside.

He pointed with the flashlight, and she hesitated long enough to hear *Swan Lake* one more time. Some women had their Taj Mahals, and some, equally beloved, had their musical waterwheels.

"Ernie, thank you for showing me that," she said after they'd gone a short way.

"You're welcome, Hannah," he answered, his voice quiet. Too quiet. Again.

The distance from Mim's to his father's house wasn't far, even in the rain. Truthfully, Hannah hated for their walk to end, but suddenly the house loomed before them, a small, low-pitched ranch house with a screened-in porch all across the front. The house was painted red and made of vertical instead of horizontal planks, with narrow wood strips covering the cracks between the planks. Hannah left the shelter of Ernie's raincoat, and the screen door squeaked loudly as he opened it for her. She waited by the inner door while he located a key that had been hidden on one of the porch rafters. The wind shifted, blowing the rain onto the porch, and he brought her close to him again while he unlocked the door. He hesitated then, and she had the distinct impression he was about to take her in his arms. Not trusting her ability to cope with that, she pushed the door open and stepped inside, waiting until Ernie felt along the inside wall for the switch and flipped the lamps on.

The interior was actually just one great big room, which blended from kitchen–dining area to living area to a bed. The floors were wood and the walls were paneled in pine. There was little in the way of decoration: no pictures, a few braided rugs scattered about. Small lamps warmed the pine paneling, giving the room a cozy, comfortable feel in spite of its austerity. Hannah glanced at the bed at the far end of the room. It was made up with a Hudson Bay blanket and no spread, the pillowcases starched and ironed—by Mim, who kept the house ready, she supposed—and embroidered in what she would guess from this distance was more of Mim's cross-stitching. She took off her rain-wet cowboy hat, but kept her jacket on while Ernie worked at the small, ornate wood stove that stood in the middle of the place. He glanced at her from time to time, but she wouldn't hold his gaze. She was afraid to do that, afraid she'd let him see the turmoil and longing she was having a devil of a time trying to hide.

He had the fire going quickly, and she came closer to get warm. Her hair was damp, and she raked her fingers through it over the heat from the stove.

"I guess you'll want to tell your dad how things are going," Ernie said as he took off his raincoat. "The phone's right there behind you. When was the last time you talked to him? He might know something by now."

Hannah didn't answer him. The last time she had talked to her father had been to notify him of her mother's death three years ago. She had felt she owed him that courtesy, but she hadn't bothered him since, and she hadn't called him about Petey, as Ernie clearly assumed.

"Hannah?"

"I can't remember his telephone number," she said truthfully enough, and she was careful not to look at him.

"I know the number—"

"Why don't you call him?" she interrupted as he tried to give it to her.

Ernie laughed. "Jake Browne's not interested in anything I've got to say, and there's no way in hell he'd stand and talk to me about Libby."

Me, either, Hannah thought, panicked now because Ernie was dialing.

"Here you go," he said, holding out the receiver. "Hannah?" he said when she didn't take it.

"Ernie, I—"

"Hannah, take the phone!"

He shoved the receiver at her in time for her to hear her father answer. She shoved it back at him.

"I can't," she said, trying to get away, but he'd caught her arm.

"What do you mean you *can't?*" She could hear her father still on the line.

"I just can't!" she cried, feeling the tears well up in her eyes. My God, was she going to stand here at her age and cry over the heartbreak caused by flagrant parental waywardness just the way Petey had?

"Hannah," Ernie said, still holding on to her. He listened to the receiver for a moment, then slammed it down. "Why didn't you talk to him?" There was enough annoyance in his voice to make her defensive.

"Listen, that call was your idea, not mine . . ."

"Why didn't you talk to him!" he yelled at her, clearly wanting to come right to the point, as usual.

"Because I never know what to call him!" she yelled back, jerking her arm free. She did *not* want to explain this, and she knew he'd try to make her do just that if she stayed. She was going to cry after all, and she didn't want him to see her do it. She headed for the door with no plan other than to get out. But he caught up with her before she could open it, holding it closed over her head.

"Hannah, this is nuts! What do you mean, you never know what to call him? He's your old man, for God's sake!"

"No, Ernie! He's not!"

CHAPTER SEVEN

"DON'T CRY."

"I'm not crying!"

"Yeah, well, what the hell do you call it?"

"What I call it is none of your business!"

"Come here—come here!"

She kept trying to bat his hands away to keep him from touching her, but he caught both her hands in his.

"Hannah, you are going to drive me crazy, you know that!"

She looked up at him. He had such a frown.

Ernie, she thought. She didn't want him to frown; he'd had enough worry with Browne women. She gave in to a sudden, insane impulse to wrap her arms around him, to take the comfort he wanted to give her, if only for a second. She needed him, and at that moment, she didn't care if he knew it. She hugged him tightly, her eyes closed, the tears squeezing out the corners and spilling down her cheeks. But she couldn't be this close to him, either. She stiffened and tried to move away from him, but he wouldn't let her go, keeping her close and making her put her head on his shoulder, holding her for what seemed a wonderfully long time.

"Hannah, I'm sorry," he whispered against her ear. "I didn't mean to do that to you. I didn't mean to make you tell me like that. A house has got to fall on me sometimes. I thought you were just being hardheaded—like Libby."

"It doesn't matter." *God, I'm as bad as Petey.*

"Yeah, it does matter. Can I ask you a question?" he said, trying to see her face.

But she was more comfortable hiding from him. "No," she said, her voice muffled in his shirt. "Yes," she amended tiredly. She was behaving like an idiot; she could spare him a question.

"Why do you think Jake's not your father? People talk, Hannah. If it's true, I never heard anything about it. And Mim—she'd know if anybody would—she's never said that."

Hannah sighed and moved out of his arms, wiping at her eyes with her fingertips. "I don't know what else it could be. How else could he live with that you-take-this-kid-and-I'll-take-that-one divorce he and my mother had? He never tried to see me. He never wrote to me. He never in my life sent me a birthday or a Christmas present. He never even sent me a card. When I was little, I used to tell people he was dead so that I wouldn't have to explain it."

"You said you moved around a lot. Maybe he didn't know where you were."

She smiled at his attempt to make her feel better. "He's a man with a lot of money, Ernie. And from what I know about Jake Browne, he would have found me if he'd wanted to."

He reached out to put his arms around her again, and she let him do it, let him hug her tightly the way he wanted to.

"Hannah, Hannah, I hate to see you so sad."

"I'm all right. Honestly. I don't dwell on it. I can't do anything about the past. I guess it's just—seeing Petey. It makes me remember, you know? I had my mother, at least. I don't think she's got either parent. So," she said, getting out of his arms again while she still could. "Is there anything hot to drink around here, do you think? Coffee? Tea?"

"I think you ought to talk to Mim," Ernie said, ignoring her attempt to change the subject.

"I don't want to talk to Mim. I told you, it doesn't matter. I'm a grown woman. Whatever I'd find out, it's too late."

"Hannah—"

"Ernie, just this once, do you think you could butt out!"

"Probably not," he said matter-of-factly. He gave her his old mischievous smile. "But I can get you some coffee." He opened a cupboard over the stove and got down a red Luzianne coffee can.

"Good," she said, forcing herself to smile in return. "You make better coffee than I do."

"Yeah, I do, don't I?" he teased gently, and it made her want to cry again. He kept glancing at her while he filled the coffee pot. "Hannah, I want to tell you why I left last night."

"I wish you wouldn't," she said tiredly.

"Yeah, I know that, but I want you to listen to me anyway."

She looked up at him. The room had grown warm, and she removed her jacket and hung it on the back of a straight chair near the stove. An old upright piano stood against one wall, and she went to look at it, admiring the heavy carving on the sides and front panel. It had been polished until it shone in the warm lamplight. Mim did indeed keep the house ready.

"My mother's," he said. "Do you play?" He was watching her. She could feel it, feel his eyes lingering on her face and breasts. It made her knees weak.

"No. I never lived in one place long enough to have a piano."

"Hannah—"

"Ernie, I really don't want to talk about last night. It—"

"Doesn't matter," he finished for her. "Yeah, you told me that before, too. Well, it matters to me."

"I don't want to get into this! What I want is for you to just . . . go. I have a lot of thinking to do. If Elizabeth doesn't show up, I have to decide what I'm going to do about Petey."

"Why are you in such a damn big hurry to put me out in the rain!"

"Ernie, I'm serious!"

"I'm serious, too. I don't want to leave, and I meant what I said to you earlier: I think I'm in love with you."

"Don't make this any worse than it already is!" she cried. "Please—"

"Hannah, I just want you to know, that's all." He set

the coffee pot on the stove and sat down on the edge of the kitchen table to take the weight off his still tender knee. She couldn't keep from looking at him, at his fine hands, long-fingered and rough-textured and gentle, and his sad eyes, and that new haircut that made him so damned handsome!

"I . . . care about you, Hannah," he said after what seemed a long time. "It scares me to death."

She looked into his beautiful eyes again. He still didn't understand the differences between Hannah and Libby Browne. "I'm not like Elizabeth," she said in spite of herself.

"No," he said quietly. "But you're not unlike her, either."

"What is that supposed to mean?"

"It means, Hannah, that I don't want to be another Rick Archer."

"What has Rick got to do with anything!"

He stared at her for a moment before he answered. The rain pelted the roof, and the room began to fill with the aroma of coffee.

"You and Rick were . . . going around together. You let him walk out of your life, Hannah. No regrets, nothing . . ."

"Ernie," she said in exasperation. So that was the reason he'd wanted to know if she'd seen Rick. He thought she'd been behaving like Elizabeth in that respect, too.

"I want to mean more to you than that, Hannah. I know all about not letting anybody get close to you because you're afraid you'll get hurt. And I know I don't fit into your life and you don't fit into mine—but I still want to mean something to you. I'm thirty-nine years old, and I'm acting like a kid. I can't eat. I can't sleep. I

think about you all the time—and I don't *want* to think
about you, dammit all! Right now, it's all I can do to
keep my hands off you, and I still want to run like hell!"

"Why don't you run, then?" she asked quietly. It
would be the best thing for both of them.

"Because I know you'd let me go. Just like you let
Archer go. It's the way you . . . handle things."

"Oh, really?" she said angrily. "And just what makes
you such an authority on human behavior!"

"Group therapy sessions at Alcoholics Anonymous,"
he said shortly. He abruptly got up and walked to the
stove, taking the coffee pot off and setting it aside. He
got down a white cup from the cupboard, and another,
but he left them both sitting and simply stood with his
back to her. She waited awkwardly, expecting him to
say something.

"Ernie?" she said when he didn't.

"What?" He moved the white coffee cup a bit to the
left, but he didn't turn around.

"Rick and I . . . weren't lovers. We weren't even
close friends. We were just professional associates—"

"Hannah, I don't want to hear this," he interrupted,
glancing at her over his shoulder.

"You don't want to hear this? Ernie, you asked me
about it on the way down here!"

"I know that," he said testily. And he was fiddling
with the coffee cups again. "I'm trying to do better by
you. I don't want to *make* you tell me anything you
don't want to tell me, like I did about your father—"

"Right! So now you won't let me tell you something
I *want* to tell you, for God's sake!"

She gave up then; she didn't want to talk anymore.
Whatever the attraction was between them, logic and
appropriateness had nothing to do with it, and whatever

they wanted to say to each other always seemed to come out wrong.

She went to him, hesitating a moment, then leaning against him, her face pressed into his back, her eyes closed. He sighed heavily, and she slid her arms around his waist, loving the scent and the feel of him and thinking this was where he'd probably break and run. Again.

"We're a pair, you know that, Hannah?" he said sadly.

"Yes, I know that. What if—" She broke off and started again. She might as well say it. "What if I think —I'm in love with you, too?" She could say it because he couldn't see her face.

"Then we're in big trouble."

He turned around, giving her a sad smile and gently brushing back her hair. "You're so pretty," he whispered, leaning down a bit to nuzzle her cheek.

"I've got freckles," she felt obliged to remind him, her eyes half closed. She could feel his breath warm against her face, feel the soft brush of his mustache.

"I love your freckles," he said, still whispering, placing a soft, lingering kiss gently on her mouth.

Oh, she thought, perhaps said. How sweet his kisses were. And how sweet it would be if just this once he didn't try to make another escape.

"Don't make me go," he whispered. The words were a soft murmuring, his mouth against hers. "Don't—"

Lord, no, she thought. That was the last thing she wanted, prudent or not, sensible or not, and in spite of what she'd just said.

"We're in big trouble," she reminded him anyway, parting her lips for him as he kissed her again.

"I know it. It's too late now."

"Is it?"

"You know damn well it is. Too late. Too soon. Everything about it's wrong," he said, his mouth coming down hard on hers.

Yes. Yes, she knew that, and the knowledge would do nothing to forestall the pain that would ultimately be hers if she continued this. Her knees were weak. The desire she'd tried to deny since the first night they'd met began once again to uncoil deep within her, leaving an aching, empty place that only he could fill. She didn't want to be hurt again, and yet she wasn't afraid. She could feel his need of her, feel it in the urgent way his mouth took hers, again and again, and in the hard pressure of his body.

Trembling. He was trembling. "Hannah," he whispered against her ear, his voice ragged with that need. She twisted her body so he could touch her breast. She wanted to be touched, wanted his warm hands on her breasts. She could feel her body opening to him, responding to the heat of the longing he generated in her like some delicate hothouse flower.

He leaned back for a moment to look at her, his eyes searching hers.

Dear God, she thought then. *He's more afraid than I am.* She could see it. He expected nothing but pain from her, the same kind of pain he'd gotten from Libby.

"I want to make love with you, Hannah."

She reached up to touch his face, but he caught her hand and pressed a soft, loving kiss into her palm. She was lost then, and she reached down to take him by the hand, to lead him to the bed with the Hudson Bay blanket at the far end of the room. He sat down on the side of the bed, then reached for her to bring her onto his lap. He held her tightly, his face between her breasts while she rested her head against his, her hands caressing the back of his neck and his shoulders. She helped him take off his denim jacket and undo the buttons on his shirt—he was wearing the old-fashioned undershirt she'd admired the night he'd brought Petey to her. No. It wasn't the undershirt she'd admired. It was the man wearing it.

Ernie.

His eyes never left hers, and from time to time he smiled that shy, quiet smile she'd seen only a very few times, the one that had left her knowing that the barriers he'd needed against her were down, the smile that left her weak with desire now. She lifted her arms for him so he could pull off her T-shirt. Underneath it she wore a soft camisole and no bra. His hands, warm and loving, gently cupped her breast, then slid up under the camisole to caress her bare skin.

"I can't believe how soft you feel," he said. "Let me look at you."

She removed the camisole herself, offering her body to him without false modesty, without shame.

"Hannah, Hannah, you are so beautiful," he whispered. "You know that, don't you?"

She hadn't known it; she was only Hannah and not Elizabeth, by any stretch of the imagination, and he'd left so abruptly before. But he made her believe it, with the tremor in his touch, with the soft, loving look and the desire in his dark eyes, with the warm press of his mouth against her skin. Her eyes closed and her hands slid into his hair as he lowered his head to circle one taut nipple with his tongue, then take it into his mouth. She felt his gentle tugging so intensely that she kept him there, giving a soft cry of pleasure as the aching, empty space in her grew hot and restless and emptier still.

They tumbled backward on the bed together, lying face to face, his legs under hers.

"The lights," she said as his warm mouth found her breasts again, moving from one to the other. "Ernie—Oh—"

He lifted his head to look at her. "I'm not hiding with you in the dark, Hannah. I want you to see me loving you."

He sat up then, removing the rest of his clothes and hers. She shivered, more from anticipation and passion than from the cool air on her bare skin. He helped her pull down the blankets and position the pillows, then stood. Hannah looked up at him. He was so beautiful, his angular male body, which she reached out to caress, his very soul, which looked out at her through such solemn eyes. She held the blankets back for him, and he stretched out beside her, careful of his knee and gathering her close to him, pressing his face into her neck for a moment, his breath ragged and warm there.

"I didn't want to leave you last night," she thought he said.

"I didn't want you to leave," she whispered, pressing a kiss against his cheek, feeling the rough stubble of his beard against her lips and loving the feel of it. Her hands rested lightly on his shoulders, and he looked at her then, smiling into her eyes.

"That's why you were holding the door open and yelling for me to get out, right?"

They laughed together, and he hugged her to him again, his hands moving slowly over her back and around to her hips, finally sliding up to cup her breasts again.

"God, you are so good for me," he said, his mouth finding hers. It left her breathless, swamped with sensations—his warm hands and the cool, crisp sheets, her desire once again spiraling upward, her worry that she wasn't as good for him as he thought. And she was afraid after all. Making love with a man for the first time meant being afraid, vulnerable—particularly *this* man. She knew how hard he'd fought not to become involved with her, and she pushed any thought of Elizabeth out of her mind. She wanted to be good for him. She wanted to hold him and to be possessed by him, and to give him more pleasure than he'd ever known. She didn't want him to be sad anymore, and she wanted to be the reason.

"My . . . sweet . . . Hannah . . ." he murmured as he held her face in his hands and kissed her, so gently and so thoroughly, eyes open so he could see her response. She outlined his lips lightly with the tip of her tongue, teasing, tasting, until he gave a soft, passion-filled moan, until his arms slid around her, and he strained to hold her closer than it was possible to be held. She reveled in the urgent pressure of his arousal against her belly and in the kisses she needed so desperately and couldn't wait to return.

"You feel so good to me," he whispered, his hands moving over her, touching her in all the places that craved his touch. "Let me love you—let me—"

"Yes!" she whispered, her voice fierce with passion. Then he was lifting her, sliding under her, bringing her leg over him.

"Hannah," he whispered, his voice as urgent as his kisses. "It's been a long time since I— I can't wait for you—"

But he was already inside her, filling the place in her body and in her soul that was meant only for him. He inhaled sharply as she took him deeply, clamping his arms around her when she fell forward onto his chest to hold her still until he could regain some element of control.

"Hannah, Hannah—" he whispered against her ear, as if her name might serve as a benediction of the need he had for her.

She wanted him; she was on fire with her need for him, and she whimpered in frustration. But then his hips thrust upward in that ancient and purpose-filled motion that changed her frustration to a pleasure so searing it was almost pain.

He didn't go to someone else last night—not Selena or Modesta or the woman with the strange voice . . .

Such pleasure. Such exquisite pleasure. Her body was suffused with it. She had never felt anything like this, and she wanted to tell him so, in soft, unrestrained words she could let spill over him as lightly as the rain that now sounded against the window at their heads.

But making love with a man for the first time was being afraid, and she tried to hide her need of him, her need to let him know that she loved him and that *she* wouldn't hurt him, ever.

Ever.

CHAPTER EIGHT

"HANNAH?"

"What?"

His arms tightened around her. "Are you . . . all right?"

"No," she said truthfully. She was still so overwhelmed by her response to him that she pressed her face into his neck and clung to him as if she were in danger of drowning. He kissed her forehead and caressed her cheek. She was cold suddenly, and she shivered against him.

"Hannah—"

"Ernie, let's don't talk, okay? I don't want to . . . talk." She had too much to sort out, too many conflicting emotions.

"Hannah, it's never been like this for me. I want to know what you're feeling—"

"No, you don't."

He hooked his fingers under her chin to make her look at him. "Yes, I do. Tell me. You're worrying me here. A lot. I didn't . . . I wasn't too rough with you or anything, was I?"

"No, no, Ernie," she whispered, hugging him tightly. "You didn't hurt me. You were—"

"What? I was what?"

She lifted her head to see his face. He had told the truth. He was worrying. "Everything," she said, staring into his eyes. "You were everything. You made me feel—"

"Hannah, don't stop now. I can't take it. Tell me."

She pressed her face into his neck again, noting amid all the turmoil she was feeling how much she loved the masculine scent of his body. She ran her hand over his chest, loving his lean, muscular feel. "As if I belong to you," she said quietly.

"What?" he asked, raising himself up so he could see her face.

She didn't repeat it, and his arms tightened around her. He kissed her forehead again, then her eyes, and finally her lips, lingering over them in a way that emptied her mind of everything but him. "I heard you," he whispered. "I just wanted to hear you say it again."

"Ernie, this doesn't mean anything if you don't want it to," she said in a rush. "I mean, it's not like you seduced me—"

"Hannah, hush!" he said, hugging her to him. "Hush!" he repeated in a rough whisper against her ear. "I've been seducing you ever since I laid eyes on you."

She couldn't keep from smiling. He could say the most tender things sometimes. "Have you?"

"You know I have. I hung around you all the time. I made you an omelet, didn't I? I took you to the rodeo. I bought you a Starlight Café hamburger—what did you think that was all about? The Starlight even has a neon sign, Hannah. A woman as crazy about neon as you are? That should have made you suspicious right there." He kissed her soundly, making her laugh.

Lord, she'd meant it when she said she felt as though she belonged to him! She wanted to lie in his arms like this forever. She wanted to hold him and touch him and make love with him. She wanted to live with him, for God's sake, somehow, somehow...

She abruptly hugged him in return, then gave him a burst of small kisses over his face and chin, then hugged him again. "I love you, Ernie," she whispered fiercely and without embarrassment.

He caught her by both shoulders to make her look at him. "Whoa! What did you say?"

She looked into his dark eyes. He'd heard her this time, too. "I said I love you. I don't *think* I love you. I don't just *possibly* love you. I love you. I... wanted you to know. In case I get busy and don't get the chance to tell you," she said, giving his earlier excuse back to him. "So there you are." She rolled onto her back and stared up at the ceiling, listening to the soft patter of the rain on the roof. She knew he wasn't ready for commitments, and he didn't say anything. Not a word.

"You didn't just go to bed with me because you're mad at Libby or anything like that, did you?" he suggested finally.

She turned her head to look at him, wondering why

that question didn't make her angry. "No," she said evenly. "Did you?"

Unfortunately, it didn't strike him in the same way. "Is that what you think!"

"I didn't until you brought it up."

"I'm crazy about you, Hannah. Don't you know that?"

"Not if you don't tell me, I don't." She propped herself up on her elbow, and she stared down at him, feeling the need to cry again. She had finally found a man she cared about, one who was scared to death of the word *love*. She bit down on her lower lip. This was no time for emotionalism. "Why?" she challenged him. "Why are you—crazy about me?"

Because I'm as close to Elizabeth as you're ever going to get?

He rolled toward her, taking her into the circle of his strong arms and legs, positioning her leg over his thigh so she wouldn't bump his knee. They lay with their heads close on the pillow, staring into each other's eyes, his big hands stroking her back. The wind had changed directions again, making the window at the head of the bed rattle.

"Because you make me feel good about myself. Because you make me feel good about being *me*—John Ernest Watson. That's something I haven't had in a long time. You know about my drinking and what I do for a living and you still make me feel like I'm somebody worth knowing. You did that right from the first, Hannah. In front of Archer—when we were standing under the umbrella that afternoon. There he was in his little executive raincoat and his little fedora and his talk-show dimples . . . but you didn't mind being seen with a rodeo clown—with me."

"Ernie, why would you think I'd mind?"

He smiled and kissed the tip of her nose. "You're pretty . . . uptown, Hannah Rose."

She looked into his eyes, thinking he had her confused with Elizabeth again. "Don't let the Perry Mason suits fool you, Watson," she whispered, and he laughed. "You know what I am, Ernie? A road vagabond who never lived in a place without a flashing neon sign."

He kissed her deeply, and her desire for him was out of hand in an instant. She clung to him, fighting down the desperation she was feeling. She shouldn't have told him she loved him, dammit! But no matter what happened, she wanted him to know she was playing for keeps.

"Hannah, Hannah," he said, against her ear. "You make me so happy. Just being with you. I don't want you to ever be sorry you let me into your life. I . . . want to tell you about Libby."

"I don't think I want to know about you and Elizabeth," she said quietly.

He took a long breath, then moved away from her and lay on his back. "You're going to hear it from somebody, Hannah. I'd rather it was me."

She nearly said again that it didn't matter. But it *did* matter. It was as much a part of John Ernest Watson as his being a bull-dodging clown, as his growing up in this place with the musical water wheel.

"I . . . know you're in love with her, Ernie."

He turned his head to look at her. "No," he answered, looking into her eyes.

"You said you wanted to marry her."

"No. Yes. I don't know—"

"Ernie," she protested. The subject was obviously a

painful one for him, and she saw no reason to put the two of them through this.

"Hannah, it's not easy to explain—"

"Fine," she said, sitting up on the side of the bed. "Then let's don't explain it."

He caught her by her arm. "Where are you going? Don't, Hannah. I *need* to tell you. I know this bed is a little too . . . crowded for you. You think it's got you and me *and* Libby in it. Hannah," he said, gathering her to him again. She resisted for a moment, then pressed her body against his, needing his warmth, his love if he had it to give.

"I don't want to talk about this."

"I want to tell you anyway. I want you to hear it, so you'll understand why I left the way I did last night." He was holding her close, his fingers gently trailing over her skin. "The night I brought Petey to you I knew how special it was going to be with us. We've got something, Hannah. You and Libby are sisters—even if the two of you did get a late start at it. I don't want that to ever be a problem between us. Do you understand?"

Instead of answering, she lifted her head to quietly kiss the places she could reach—his shoulder, the side of his neck, his cheek, his lips. She gave a soft sigh. "I'm listening," she said, because she had no viable alternative. And she was afraid again, afraid that hearing the details of his relationship with Elizabeth would convince her how futile her loving him was going to be.

He suddenly lifted her up so she lay on top of him. It was as if he wanted to be able to touch her freely for a moment, as if he wanted to feel her as close to him as possible before he told her about Elizabeth. His warm, rough hands stroked her body and held her tightly before moving her beside him again. He covered them both carefully with the Hudson Bay blanket, and he lay with her in his arms, one hand quietly caressing the top of her head. She closed her eyes, savoring this closeness with him. She loved him so!

"Mim calls Libby a . . . stray-away child, after some mountain song she heard when she went visiting the North Carolina Cherokee relatives years ago," he said after a time. "Some children are born like that, she says, always into trouble. *Always*. They never stay where you put them, and God and all his angels can't keep up with them. Somebody down here has to do that. Which is fine for the stray-away, but I can tell you it's damn hard on the keeper."

He gave a sharp sigh, and she could feel the tension in him.

"Go on," she prompted. If she had to hear it, she wanted to hear it and be done with it.

"That's what I am to Libby. Her keeper. I . . . always have been. Ever since I can remember. One thing after another. You wouldn't believe the things I've taken the blame for. She crippled one of Jake's prize quarter horses one time. My old man and Uncle Michael knew I wouldn't ride an animal into the ground like that. They both went to Jake about it, but I'd . . . 'confessed,' you see. Took all three of us five years to pay for that horse. The crazy thing was, I couldn't stay mad at her—no matter how hard I tried. She was always so sorry afterward, and we both knew it was just a matter of time until she did something else just as crazy or worse. God, I hated it—hated her, too, a lot of the time. And I . . . loved her . . . the way a kid still loves a parent who beats him." He pressed his cheek against the top of her head for a moment. "The way you still love Jake."

"I don't even know him," she protested.

"Yeah, but that doesn't keep you from loving him. Trying to deal with him wouldn't make you cry if you didn't."

She had nothing to say to that, and he took her hand in his, holding it to his chest. "After I moved to New Mexico, I'd go a long time without seeing Libby or hearing from her. And then out of the blue she'd call or she'd come on the bus. She was always in the middle of some crisis when she did that. One crisis was too bad even for Mim to know about, but Libby never seemed to mind if I knew her . . . secrets. I'd lend her money, let her hide out for a while, run interference with Mim— whatever it took. About five years ago, she came to see me again—in Chimayo. Mac's mother had a little house there—she was a painter, and she used it as her studio. It's a pretty place; it's adobe, with an adobe wall around it. You'd like it, I think," he added, pressing a kiss on her forehead.

I would if you were there, she thought.

"Libby was in another crisis, but she wouldn't tell me what it was. She was . . . different, quieter. She kept looking at me like she'd just found out something she didn't know before. She finally told me what it was. She suddenly realized how much she 'needed' me—'loved' me. We were never lovers," he continued. "Until then," he qualified, and Hannah's spirits plummeted. She had known as much, of course, but it still hurt to hear it.

"She . . . stayed with me for a week in that little house in Chimayo. And then I woke up one morning and she was gone. She left me a letter, believe it or not. She even explained. She'd been living with a man named O'Day. She was pregnant. She wasn't sure he'd want to marry her, and she'd needed some time just to forget. She thanked me for that—for helping her forget. That's how I know Petey isn't my kid. Libby married Petey's father a week later."

"Ernie—"

"There's more, Hannah. I want you to hear it. I stood there and read that letter. Over and over, but it still said the same thing. I . . . couldn't believe it. My pride was hurt, and I was furious with myself because I knew better. I *knew* better, and I still let her do that to me; and worse than that, I'd been dumb enough to tell people we were getting married. People were going to *know* what a damn fool John Ernest Watson was.

"But Libby didn't make me start drinking. I was . . . humiliated, and drinking was the way I chose to deal with it. I wanted a hole to hide in and I found it. The funny thing is, I never was much of a social drinker before then. I could take it or leave it. But I started making the rounds, hitting all the honky-tonks and looking for women who'd make me feel better for a little while at least. It got to the point where I was staying more drunk than sober, and all of a sudden I couldn't just take it or leave it anymore. I knew I couldn't, but I lied to myself and to anybody who tried to talk to me about it. Two-thirds of what happened to me then I don't even remember. You know your moment of truth? Well, I was doing everything I could to hide from mine. But . . . I had some good friends. Mac McDade and his old man. *My* old man. They got ahold of me one day, and they made me look at myself, made me see what they were seeing. They took me to a place where I could get some help—hell, they even went in with me. So now I go to AA, and I take life one day at a time, and I—" He didn't go on, and she lifted her head to look at him. "Until she left Petey with me, I'd only seen her once since that time in Chimayo."

"At Mim's," Hannah said.

He frowned. "How did you know that?"

"I saw the picture in Mim's album." The picture that showed so clearly that he'd once again forgiven Elizabeth.

The phone rang sharply, and because she was closest, Hannah moved to answer it, taking Ernie's plaid shirt with her and slipping it on. She turned around to look at him as she picked up the receiver, smiling a bit at his overt appraisal of her lack of attire.

He cares about me. He's crazy about me. He thinks *he loves me . . .*

He folded his arms behind his head and gave her a playful wink. "You're doing a lot for my shirt there, Hannah."

"Hello?" she said into the phone, her smile broadening. Regardless of what he felt for her, he had a way of making her feel good about herself, too, for all his long history with Elizabeth.

There was silence on the other end of the line.

"Hello?" she said again, listening a moment for some clue as to whether anyone was there. She heard nothing, and she frowned at the receiver a moment, then hung up.

"Who knows we're here besides Mim?" she asked.

"Half of Tahlequah, I imagine." He sat up on the side of the bed and put on his jeans, then went to work on the wood stove. She watched him, brazenly admiring the ripple of muscles in his back and arms as he stoked the fire. "Come here," he said when he had the fire burning again.

He didn't have to coax her; she went to him, kissing

him on the neck and cheek and pushing up the long sleeves of his plaid shirt before she wrapped her arms around him. He sat down on the chair where she'd hung her jacket and took her into his lap, sliding his hand up under the shirt to caress her bare hip. "I am never going to get enough of you," he said gruffly, his mouth seeking hers.

The phone rang again, and he sighed heavily.

"I'll get it this time," he said, shifting her off his lap.

There was no one on the line. Ernie broke the connection and dialed a number. "Mim," he said after a moment, "did you just call? No, nothing. You haven't heard anything, have you? No, I'm going to stay here tonight with Hannah."

Hannah raised her eyebrows a bit at that last part, and Ernie grinned.

"Yeah," he said after a moment, and then, "Hi, Pete! Yeah, Anna-Hannah's here. Has she got on her nightie?" He looked Hannah and his plaid shirt over carefully, making her grin. "Nope. No nightie. Did you brush your teeth? Good girl. Don't you go eating cake, now, after you've got your teeth brushed, okay? Yeah," he said, beckoning to Hannah, who was already coming closer. "Give me a kiss, then. Here's Anna-Hannah."

"Hello, dear sweet Petey," Hannah said, taking the phone.

"Hello, dear wheat, Anna . . . Hannah," Petey responded, punctuating it with the soft giggle Hannah loved. Hannah stood in the circle of Ernie's arms, leaning against his bare chest, lifting her mouth a bit to receive the soft kiss he was about to offer her.

"Are you ready for bed?" Hannah asked, trying not to laugh at Ernie who was nodding vigorously. "Kiss me good night, then. I'll see you in the morning. Pleasant dreams . . . good night . . . dear sweet Petey."

Ernie took the receiver out of her hand, making sure Petey had hung up before he replaced it. "I love that little kid," he said unnecessarily. Petey was all tangled up in the reason for his pain over Elizabeth, Hannah thought, but because of the kind of man he was, he clearly loved her anyway. She looked up at him, and he smiled, but the smile didn't quite reach his dark eyes. Elizabeth was still there, still crowding both of them, and he was still worrying.

"Ernie," she whispered, reaching up to touch his face, to brush her thumb over his raggedy mustache. He pressed his cheek into the palm of her hand, and the smile faded. He leaned down to give her another kiss, a kiss that suddenly accelerated, making him give a soft moan as his lips ground into hers. He kissed her until she was breathless, until she realized she was never going to get enough of him, either.

He finally broke away, his breath quick and warm against her ear. "I care about you, Hannah. I can't believe this. You don't know how hard I tried . . ." He didn't go on, burying his face in her shoulder.

"Not to," she finished for him. "Ernie, I'm not afraid of this. I'm not." It wasn't quite the truth. She was afraid, more for him than for herself. He kissed her again, then lifted her up and carried her to the bed.

"Damn this knee!" he said in exasperation as he tried to put her down. "The doctor left the clamps in too long because he thought I'd be back rodeoing before I was supposed to. He nearly killed me getting them all out."

"Maybe *I* should carry *you,*" she suggested, and they both laughed, heads together. He set her down awkwardly, then tumbled onto the bed alongside her with some fancy maneuvering to protect his knee. He gave a loud groan and turned his head to look at her.

"Is this romantic, Hannah Rose, or what?" he asked a bit wearily, grinning and gingerly trying to coax his knee into working again. "I've got something to ask you," he said after a moment.

"What?"

"Help me get my pants off!"

He punctuated that request with an onslaught of wild kissing and tickling, rolling her onto him and off again and making her squeal.

"Ernie! Wait—your knee!" she protested, but she was loving every minute of it, and he knew it.

"Now, there you go, Hannah. Trying to change the subject just like you did the first time I tried to get you to take my pants off."

They ended up with her on top of him again, his shirt well off her shoulders as he nibbled at her neck and the soft swell of her breasts.

"You were right," she said, still laughing. "We can't be alone together without getting into—*trouble*—Ernie!"

"You're not alone," Elizabeth said quietly.

Hannah jumped, struggling to get out of Ernie's arms, but he wouldn't let her go. She would always be grateful to him for that—that he didn't cheapen their relationship by behaving like a man caught with his hand in the cookie jar. He held her still, reaching up to touch her cheek and looking into her eyes before he let her go. He sat up on the side of the bed, hunting for his discarded undershirt. He put it on, and he said nothing, seemingly unmoved by Elizabeth's tearstained face. She'd had her blond hair cut in a chic new style, but she was much more disheveled than was fashionable. She stood there, a tragic figure dressed all in black, rain-wet and distraught. God, she was beautiful, even like this, Hannah thought.

"I wanted you to look after Petey for me, Hannah, but this isn't what I had in mind." Her voice quivered with emotion, and she put her hand to her eyes for a moment to regain control. "Hannah, what are you *doing?*"

"Have you seen Petey?" Ernie interrupted. He stood up and handed Hannah her clothes, then walked the length of the room to the kitchen, setting the coffee pot back on the stove.

"No, I haven't seen her!" Elizabeth cried, following him, leaving Hannah with what little privacy there was to put her clothes on. "I've been trying to find out what's going on. I went looking for you at the Cowtown rodeo, Ernie. They said they thought you were living with Hannah. I couldn't believe it! I called her place twice today. She said you weren't there and she wasn't sure when you'd be back." Her eyes flew to Hannah. "I gave you those false names because I didn't want you to know it was me," she snapped before Hannah could accuse her of anything. "Are you and Ernie living together?"

"No, Elizabeth," Hannah said, offering Ernie his shirt. He shook his head, and she laid it across the disheveled bed. "Ernie's been helping me look after Petey. You called here, too, didn't you?"

"Yes, I did. And then I came over. I wanted to see for myself. It's a good thing I didn't get here any later, isn't it?" She smiled through her tears, and Hannah realized that, for whatever reason, Elizabeth needed to think she'd come in time to keep her and Ernie from becoming lovers.

"What are you going to do about Petey?" Hannah asked. She wasn't going to be put on the defensive, no matter how defensive she felt.

"Why? Do you want to take *her* away from me, too?" Elizabeth said sarcastically.

"Libby, that's enough," Ernie said.

"That's enough?" she said incredulously, turning on him. "Oh, is it really? What do you think this is, anyway, Ernie? Hannah is just like everybody else. People are jealous of me. They want what I've got. They *always* want what I've got—she's pathetic. She wouldn't want you if you didn't belong to me, don't you know that?"

"Whatever is between Hannah and me has nothing to do with you."

She looked from one of them to the other, tears welling up in her eyes.

"You can't have him, Hannah," she said, her voice childlike and quivering. "You can't!" Tears spilled down her face. "Please," she said pitifully. "Please! You took our mother, Hannah. Don't take him, too!"

Hannah went to her, because she couldn't do otherwise. Mim had been right: Elizabeth was a stray-away, and her lost look worked on Hannah, as it always did. She understood Ernie's relationship with her sister better than he knew.

She put her hand out. "Elizabeth?"

But Elizabeth didn't want to be touched. She stood rigidly in the middle of the room, her arms wrapped round her body.

"What's wrong with us, Hannah? We're *both* pathetic. We don't know how it's done, do we? I can't keep from marrying all the time, and you won't marry at all."

"Elizabeth," Hannah said again, reaching out to her.

"No! I'm better off than you are, Hannah. I'm not afraid to take a chance. You think for a minute Nathan Williamson would have gotten away from me if I'd loved him the way you did? I'd have promised him any-thing—*anything*. Wait. Wait—Hannah, you're not in love with Ernie now, are you? Oh, poor Hannah. You don't know what you've missed, Hannah Rose. He's a *wonderful* lover . . ." She laughed suddenly. "My God, wait until Daddy finds out John Ernest Watson tried to bed his other daughter!"

"Libby, I said that's enough!" Ernie barked. "What do you want!"

"Ernie, why are you doing this! Why are you stand-ing up for her!" She swayed on her feet. "Ernie—" She held out her hands to him. "I need—I have to talk to you. I *have* to. Please. Alone. It's bad this time, Ernie. My poor Petey . . ."

She swayed, and he caught her before she fell. Han-nah brought the chair with her jacket hanging on it, but Elizabeth wouldn't sit down. Her head fell forward onto Ernie's shoulder, and she reached up to lock her arms around his neck.

"Libby, have you taken anything?" he asked her.

She giggled. "Me? You're the one who has a prob-lem with a controlled substance, Ernie."

"Libby, have you taken anything!" He tried to get her arms from around his neck.

"No! I swear! I'm just so tired, Ernie. Please, please, we have to talk. Alone."

He glanced at Hannah, shooting her a look she'd seen before: *Trust me.*

This was like a scene from a very bad melodrama, Hannah thought. She turned abruptly away and went to stand at the kitchen sink and stare out the window. She could see nothing but her own reflection in the dark, rain-spattered glass, and she stood there trying not to listen to their conversation. She couldn't hear the words; she could only tell that Elizabeth was still pleading and that Ernie—

So, Hannah thought suddenly. This was how he'd learned to handle Petey so easily. He'd had a lifetime of learning—with her mother. Hannah looked over her shoulder at them. Ernie spoke to Elizabeth gently, and she clung to him.

"Did you lie to me?" she heard Elizabeth say distinctly. "Did you? You said you'd always love me. *Always!*"

"Libby—"

"Did you?"

He hesitated only a moment, then shook his head. No.

No, Hannah repeated over and over in her mind. *No.*

CHAPTER NINE

"HANNAH?" Ernie said behind her. She knew he was there—she could see his reflection in the kitchen window—but she didn't turn around.

"I'm . . . going to take Libby to Jake's."

She nodded and sidestepped him to take the coffee pot off the stove. It was ludicrous how many times this coffee had been heated when no one was ever going to drink it. He touched her arm, and she stiffened, so he took his hand away.

"Hannah, I—"

"I was thinking we didn't get Cowpoke out of the truck, did we?" she interrupted, turning around to look at him. She'd promised him their being together—making love together—wouldn't mean anything if he didn't want it to, and she'd meant it.

"Hannah—"

"I was thinking I'd walk back and see—take it in to Mim if it's still in the truck. Petey might wake up and need—"

"Hannah!" he whispered fiercely. "I want you to wait here."

She looked up at him, letting her eyes linger in his. Dear God, how she wanted to be angry with him: *You got all tangled up with me when you knew better, Ernie. When you knew I was already looking into your eyes too long, and you knew how easy it was for us to be together and to talk to each other and to take care of Petey. You wanted to run, so why didn't you? Why didn't you run!*

But she made no accusations, said nothing.

"Wait for me. I mean it!"

"All right," she said quietly, and she looked away from his eyes.

"Promise me!"

She made herself look at him. "I . . . promise," she lied, when she'd thought she would never, ever lie to him. She had but one consuming thought: to get to the Tahlequah bus station, if there was one. There was only one way she could survive this situation, and that was by getting out of it as soon as possible.

"No, hell, you don't!" he whispered, grabbing her arm. "Don't you do this, Hannah. Not now—"

"Ernie?" Elizabeth called to him.

"I told you how it was, Hannah," he said.

"Yes," she agreed. He'd told her. He'd told her what she already knew, and she'd still let herself love him. She managed a small smile. "Take care of her, Ernie," she said, nodding in Elizabeth's direction. "If I can do anything—look after Petey or anything, I will." She was letting him go, and he knew it.

"Hannah—" he began, but Elizabeth called him again. She was crying harder now, leaning against the front door, one hand outstretched.

Ernie turned abruptly and led her outside, letting the squeaky screen door bang hard behind them.

Hannah stood quietly. She could hear the rain on the roof, the hiss of the coffee heating, the wind. She drank the coffee after all, sitting alone in the house and finally falling asleep in a bed that was no longer crowded. She woke up cold and lonely just before daylight. The rain had stopped, and she lay there trying to make plans. She had wanted to leave immediately, to hitch a ride into Tahlequah, to walk if she had to, anything to get away, but once again she found herself bound by her responsibility to a child. *Petey.* What was going to happen to her? Would she stay with Mim, go to her grandfather Jake's, or be off again with Elizabeth, who couldn't even look after herself, much less take care of a child. Marriage wasn't the only thing she and Elizabeth couldn't manage—neither of them seemed to have a gift for mothering, either.

She shivered, then maneuvered until she had the blanket doubled and tried to get warm, toying with the idea of getting up and starting a fire. But she wouldn't need a fire. She wouldn't be here that long. When it was light enough, she'd gather up her things and walk to Mim's. She'd see Petey and say her good-byes. Surely someone would take her to the nearest station. She had enough money to get back to Dallas alone, and she certainly didn't want to make that long trip with Ernie.

She closed her eyes. She hadn't cried, not at all,

although she had never in her life felt so sad. She supposed that the lack of tears had to do with her sense of resignation at having made such an ill-advised choice when, like Ernie, she had known better. Still, she couldn't say she was sorry. Elizabeth had been wrong about one thing: Hannah hadn't been afraid to take the chance, and she was never going to regret having let John Ernest Watson into her life. She suddenly smiled, thinking of him. That was the kind of man he was, the kind a woman smiled about when she knew he wasn't looking.

She abruptly sat up on the side of the bed. She'd had enough of this. She built a fire in the stove, after all, waited until the house was warm, and then took a long shower. She felt a little better when she came out of the bathroom—until she saw Mim Swimmer on the porch. She sighed heavily and opened the door ahead of her knock.

"John Ernest sent me," Mim said without prelude, stepping in out of the wind. She turned around so Hannah could help her off with her coat. "I hope that look you're wearing is for the message and not the messenger," she added as Hannah hung the coat on a peg by the door.

Hannah made no comment, but Mim wasn't about to let her get away with that.

"Aren't you going to ask why he sent me?"

"I know why. He's in the habit of looking after Browne women and he can't get out of it."

"No," Mim said matter-of-factly as she looked around the place. "I'll make some coffee."

"I don't want coffee."

"Then I'll make it for myself. It's cold out today and I need it."

She left Hannah standing and went about the business of coffee-making.

"Mim, I'm sorry. I'm being rude."

"Yes," Mim said without looking up. "Not without provocation, but rude nevertheless."

Hannah sighed and began gathering up her things and stuffing them into her duffel bag, glancing up once because Mim wasn't stopping at just coffee. She was frying bacon and scrambling eggs and making toast as well.

"Life is life, Hannah," she said. "You can't change one thing about it. You can only face what you have to face with your stomach full. Now, come and set two places."

Hannah hesitated for a moment, then gave in, because it seemed easier than arguing. She got the plates out of the cabinet Mim showed her, and she found, to her surprise, that she was actually hungry by the time Mim brought breakfast to the table.

"Is Petey all right?" Hannah asked after a long time of eating in silence.

"Petey is fine. It's John Ernest you should be asking about."

"Mim—"

"Unless you're like Elizabeth, and you don't care whether he's all right or not."

Hannah looked at the older woman. Yes, she wanted to know about Ernie, but she couldn't make herself admit it. "Is . . . Elizabeth all right?"

"No, but this is her own doing, and whatever's wrong this time, she's not telling. Jake and Ernie are trying to get it out of her, and she's trying to drag Ernie into it with everything she's got. She'll do it, too, if you're not careful."

"I don't have anything to do with this."

"Of course you do. Why else would I be here?"

"I'm sure I don't know," Hannah said, and Mim gave a small smile.

"And whose fault is that? Sometimes you have to dig in and ask questions, Hannah. Elizabeth is like my own baby. I've looked after her since the day she was born. I love her, but I'm not blind to her faults. Now, John Ernest—he's like my own baby, too. You never saw a better child. I don't mean he didn't get into things. He did. He was a rascal—*is* a rascal, as you probably well know. But he cares about people. He always has. It's the way he is. It's why he took to being a rodeo clown the way he did, and it's why he's always looked after Elizabeth. It's why she was able to tear him apart. There's no way in this world he'd walk away from somebody who asked him for help, no matter what it cost him . . . and that's why I'm so worried about him."

"Ernie's not drinking, is he?"

"If he isn't, it's no thanks to you."

"To me? I haven't—"

"You're the one who's breaking his heart."

"I'm not breaking his heart! Mim, I don't think you understand the situation here—"

"I understand what I understand," she said, handing Hannah a slice of toast. In her agitation, Hannah took it. "Eat," Mim admonished.

"I don't want to eat! I want to know about Ernie!"

"Good," Mim praised her, but she didn't tell her anything.

"Mim—"

"Eat," she insisted. "Then we'll talk. Eat!" she said again when Hannah was about to protest. "I'm an old woman. I didn't walk all this way over wet ground in a freezing wind to have you not eat the best breakfast you'll find from here to Dallas. And while you're eating, you can think."

"About what?" Hannah said, taking a bite of toast in spite of herself.

"John Ernest," Mim said pointedly. And she got up from the table and moved her chair closer to the stove, sitting quietly while Hannah picked over her food all she was going to.

"So," she said when Hannah reluctantly dragged her chair over to join her. "What are you going to do about John Ernest?"

Hannah frowned. She could see well enough where Ernie had gotten his penchant for *not* working up to something. "Nothing," she said flatly.

"Why not?"

"He loves Elizabeth."

"Yes," Mim agreed. "So what are you going to do about John Ernest?" she repeated.

"Mim—"

"What are you going to do about him?"

"I'm not going to do anything, for God's sake! He loves Elizabeth!"

"And so you'll just give up."

"Mim," Hannah said in exasperation, "I . . . don't have a choice. Elizabeth is—" She didn't go on.

"What is she, Hannah? Tell me."

Hannah looked into Mim's dark eyes. She didn't want to be in the conversation, but she answered anyway. "Beautiful. Wild. Fiery. No man's ever going to tame her, but they all want to try. I can't compete with her."

"A man needs a certain fire in the woman he loves, Hannah, but that fire should warm his heart, not destroy him. John Ernest has had nothing but pain from Elizabeth. And she's about to hurt him again—by making you run away and leave him."

"Mim, you don't understand! I did the wrong thing. I knew about Ernie and Elizabeth. I knew she counted on him, and he told me the first night we met that he'd wanted to marry her. I pretended it didn't matter. I let myself get—"

"He loves you," Mim interrupted.

"He hasn't said so," Hannah countered.

"He hasn't said so?" Mim asked incredulously. "Then what am I doing here? What is he doing calling me after midnight and telling me to come over and talk to you as soon as I can? He's got his hands full with Elizabeth, and he's worried to death you don't understand—which I'm thinking you don't. Do you love John Ernest, or don't you?"

"Yes!" Hannah cried, her eyes filling with tears. "Yes—"

"Then I'm going to give you a piece of advice, Hannah. I'm going to tell you what you'll have to put up with if you stay with him. Yes, he'll help Elizabeth if she comes asking. And he'll help anybody else who comes asking, too. If he needs to, he'll take *your* last dime to get some down-on-his-luck cowboy out of jail. And then, while you're being all mad about that, he'll be gone all night because he's driving that same rounder a couple hundred miles so he can see his children. And if that's not bad enough, he'll expect you to drop everything and go with him. You're going to have strangers sitting at your supper table and sleeping on your couch at all hours. It's not that he's weak or that he lets people take advantage of him. It's just the way he *is*. His idea of taking you out on the town will be some hole-in-the-wall where you have to eat standing up and the waitresses wear hair curlers—because the people there are decent and hardworking and the conversation, not necessarily the food, is good."

Hannah suddenly grinned, thinking of the Starlight Café. "I've almost been there already."

"See?" Mim said. "He *likes* people, Hannah, and he doesn't care what they've got or what they can do for him. He's never met a stranger in his life, and if you love him, you'll have to put up with it, because you'll never change him. If you can't do that, then I want you to leave him here and now. Don't hurt him, because he's had enough of that. He's a good man, for all his troubles with drink, and he needs you, but if you love him and you *want* to stay with him, you're going to have to trust him to take care of his problem with Elizabeth himself. You can't help him with it—except to wait while he does it and not add to his troubles. He's got a lot to settle with her, and he knows he's going to have to settle it if the two of you are going anywhere together. You have to just—*love* him, Hannah. And you have to wait."

"I'm not very good at waiting."

"So John Ernest told me."

"What is that supposed to mean?"

"I don't know," Mim assured her. "He didn't have time to talk much. He only said that you let go of things that hurt you, and he thinks it's got something to do with Jake."

"Oh, he did," Hannah said a bit testily.

"Yes. He said that. And he said to tell you that he'd wrapped you in chains . . ." Mim frowned. "Now I can't remember." She thought for a moment. "Light . . ."

"Chains as light as gossamer," Hannah said quietly, looking away.

"Yes. I guess he thought you'd understand what that meant."

Hannah didn't reply. She understood, not that it mattered. It wasn't going to work out for the two of them, no matter how much they both might want it, and there was no point in thinking otherwise. The telephone rang, and she let Mim answer it, hoping it wasn't Ernie and hoping just as hard that it was.

Mim looked around at her sharply. "Yes, she's here. Do you want to talk to her?"

Hannah waited, her heart beginning to pound.

"No," Mim said. "I haven't. Because that's the truth. She's been having breakfast with me. Do you want to ask her?"

She abruptly held the phone away from her ear. "That was Jake," she said, hanging up. "He can't find Ernie."

CHAPTER TEN

"Is ELIZABETH—did he take Elizabeth with him?"

She was taking Mim's advice about one thing. She was going to dig in and ask questions.

"Yes," Mim said, putting on her coat. "That's why Jake called. He thought they might be here with you."

"He—Jake—didn't want to talk to me, did he?" she asked unnecessarily.

"No, Hannah, he didn't. He's worried about Elizabeth."

"Where do you think they are?"

"Oh, honey, I don't know. More than likely John Ernest and Jake had words, and Jake had him thrown off the place, not thinking Elizabeth would go with him. I'm going over there and see what I can do." She reached up to pat Hannah's cheek. "I guess that leaves you with the dirty dishes. I need to run by and make sure Michael and Petey are all right. Don't go back to Dallas yet, Hannah. Wait for John Ernest. I want to be able to tell him that when I see him—that you're waiting."

"Mim, there's no point in that." *Especially now.*

"Wait, Hannah. Be strong. Waiting will cost you nothing, and it may make all the difference in your happiness—and John Ernest's."

Mim looked at her expectantly for a reply, and when she didn't give it, she hugged Hannah tightly. "You won't go without seeing Petey?"

"No," Hannah said. She could make that promise. "I'll see Petey before I leave."

The house was suddenly too small after Mim's departure. Hannah put on her jacket and walked outside, leaving the dirty dishes. The sun was bright and the wind cold. She walked around the place, trying not to think about Ernie and seeing him in this place just the same. He'd grown up here until his mother's death; it was here that he'd first met and loved Elizabeth. She walked down to the pond, noticing the many dogwood trees that bordered the property. *It must be beautiful here in the spring,* she thought, turning her head sharply at the first notes of *Swan Lake.* She smiled. What a tender gesture that was. A musical waterwheel. She had no doubt at all that Ernie's mother had loved it.

She stood at the water's edge, watching the wind blow ripples across the pond. She could hear the sound of traffic in the distance, and crows. Her nose was getting cold, and she turned her back to the wind.

John Ernest Watson.

Oh, Ernie . . .

She stood there remembering the feel of being wrapped in that raincoat with him, his body hard and warm against hers, and the endearing way he'd wanted to show her this place.

She suddenly remembered Elizabeth's question: *Did you lie to me?*

No, he'd told her. *No.*

Mim could be matter-of-fact about his loving Elizabeth. Hannah couldn't. It hurt. And she knew that what Mim had said about him was true. John Ernest Watson was a caring man. That was the reason he'd stayed and helped her look after Petey in the first place, and that was the reason he'd sent Mim to make sure she was all right now.

She looked up at the sound of a truck coming too fast—recklessly fast—down the long dirt drive that led in from the highway. The truck was new and shiny black, but the driver paid no attention at all to the recent rain, hitting the potholes hard and sending a shower of water and mud in his wake. He turned sharply toward the house, pulling close to the porch.

He was already getting back into the truck when Hannah reached the yard. She stood squinting in the bright sunlight, trying to keep her hair from blowing into her eyes, waiting for Jake Browne to tell her what he was doing here.

He was a tall man, his face weathered and ageless from being out in the sun. He was in his work clothes, jeans and boots and a fleece-lined denim jacket. He wore a cowboy hat with a silver and turquoise band and, as incongruous as it seemed to Hannah, a diamond ring on his left little finger. She could still see much of the young man from the picture in Mim's album.

He caught sight of her just as she was about to slam

the truck door closed. "I didn't think anyone was here," he said, clearly startled but recovering quickly. His eyes traveled over her face, but she had no idea what he was thinking. She wondered if he even knew who she was.

"No one is," she answered, "except me." She shivered in a blast of wind. "I'm going inside. You can come in if you want."

She left him sitting there, half in half out of his mud-splattered truck. She expected him to leave, but he didn't. He got out and slammed the door closed, following her onto the porch—probably because he wanted to see for himself whether she was hiding Ernie and Elizabeth.

"I'm looking for Watson," he said as they went into the house. He was close enough for her to decide that he smelled exactly the way she'd always thought her father, the rancher, would smell: a bit like horses and stale pipe tobacco.

"Yes, I know. I haven't seen him since he took Elizabeth home." She shrugged her coat off and hung it on the peg. "There's some coffee, but it's cold. I'll heat it up if you want." It surprised her how calm she sounded. Perhaps it surprised him as well. He certainly looked as if he'd never even considered the possibility of her offering him a cup of coffee.

"I—all right. If it's not too much trouble."

"It's not any trouble." She set about warming the coffee. She felt no obligation to play hostess other than that, and she left him standing awkwardly while she began to gather up the dirty dishes from her breakfast with Mim.

"They tell me you're a . . . career woman," he said after a time, dragging a chair away from the stove and sitting at the kitchen table.

"I am. But don't worry. Mim made the coffee."

He almost smiled, and the conversation lagged again.

"Look," Hannah said finally. "You don't have to hang around here for the coffee if you don't want to. I don't know where Ernie would go with Elizabeth—"

"Is that what your mama taught you?" he broke in. "Offer somebody coffee and then try to run him off?"

"No, that's not what she taught me. She taught me not to let anything suffer if I could help it."

"Even me," he suggested.

"Even you," she agreed.

"Watson tells me you think I'm not your daddy," he said out of the clear blue.

"If you are, you're a damn poor excuse for one," she answered, and he laughed.

"You don't mind telling me to my face, do you?"

"Not much, no."

He looked at her thoughtfully. "You don't look like her—your mama."

"No," Hannah said, turning away from him to get the coffee pot. She poured him a cup, wondering where this conversation was leading.

"You look like *my* mama," he said, and she looked up at him. "You and Petey both. Yeah, you're mine, and yeah, I'm late on being a father to you. Nothing I can do about it now, though." He took the cup she offered him.

"There's something you could do for Elizabeth."

"Now, look!" he said, slamming the cup down on the table. "I'm getting a little bit tired of outsiders like you and Watson trying to tell me what I ought to be doing about my daughter!"

"Fine!" Hannah said. "But Elizabeth needs you to love her enough to get her some help instead of indulging her every whim. And outsiders or not, Ernie and I are the ones she trusted to take care of Petey, aren't we?"

He got up from the table. She shouldn't have said that, but it was too late now. She knew by virtue of the fact that he'd come here how worried he must be.

"Much obliged for the coffee—and you know Watson's left you high and dry, don't you? Damned if I know what the two of you see in that scamp."

"He's a good man," Hannah said quietly.

"Girl!" her father said in exasperation. "He ain't nothing! He ain't got nothing and he ain't ever going to."

"Being a success has got nothing to do with having money," Hannah said. "My mother taught me that, too."

They stared at each other—until Jake Brown abruptly turned and left, letting the screen door bang behind him in much the same way as Ernie had. Hannah stood at the window and watched him drive away, with mud flying and with no regard for new tires and shiny black paint.

I have got to get out of here.

She closed her eyes and took a deep breath.

Ernie, where are you?

She looked around the room. She'd straighten up the place, and then she'd see Petey, and then she would leave. That's all there was to it.

She washed the few dishes and made the bed and closed the dampers on the stove, rushing around as if she truly had to catch a bus. She gathered up the last of her things and stuffed them into the duffel bag. If she put some distance between herself and all this, maybe she could decide what to do next.

The telephone rang, and she stumbled over her duffel bag in her haste to answer it.

"Please be Ernie," she said out loud, not even realizing she'd said it.

It was Mim, sounding upset and out of breath.

"Hannah—Jake was here. I was afraid you'd gone thumbing along the highway—"

"Mim, have you heard from Ernie?" she interrupted.

"Yes. He called just now. He couldn't talk but a minute—and then Jake came." Mim stopped to catch her breath. "Ernie wanted me to tell you something."

"Mim, what?"

"He said to ask you to wait for him. And then he said, 'No, ask her to *please* wait.' He said he'd come there as soon as he could."

She didn't say anything.

"Hannah, did you hear me?"

The silence lengthened.

"Hannah?"

"Yes," she said finally.

"Hannah, honey, I don't want you to feel you have no choice. Michael and I will take you back to Dallas if you want to go. And I told Ernie that."

She closed her eyes for a moment and pressed her fingers against the tight circle of pain that a restless night and a worry-filled day had centered in the middle of her forehead. "No, Mim. I'm . . . going to stay here. For a little while."

She could hear Mim's sigh of relief.

"Hannah, you know I think it's the best thing for you and John Ernest both. You'll find plenty to eat in the refrigerator. And will you walk over here if you get lonesome?"

"I—yes. I'll walk over. And you'll call me if you

hear anything? And Mim," she added. "Could I talk to Petey?"

"Jake took her with him, Hannah. He's her grandfather. I couldn't say no."

Hannah sat for a long while after she'd hung up the telephone—not an easy thing to do when all she wanted was to be gone. She just didn't know what Ernie wanted from her . . . again. Elizabeth needed help, needed Ernie; she knew that. It was just that she was afraid—not of losing him precisely, since she'd never really had him. She was afraid of losing a chance with him. That was all they had, a chance, a beautiful, golden chance to go through life together, even if it meant putting up with strangers on the couch and middle-of-the-night drives to take some hard-luck cowboy someplace he needed to go. She smiled to herself. During her gypsy childhood, there had been any number of times when she and her mother had needed a friendly couch or middle-of-the-night transportation themselves, plenty of times when they'd arrived at some out-of-the-way motel to find a No Vacancy sign when they'd had neither the money nor the strength to go on. The Alma, the Bluebird of Happiness, the Evening Breeze. Beautiful neon names. But her mother had never been discouraged. If you were tired, you rested. If you needed money, you went to work. *Somebody always needs a good waitress, Hannah Rose*.

She suddenly frowned. Unfortunately, somebody didn't always need a good television person. One scratched to find a position, and one continued scratching to hold on to it. She'd been indulging herself in the fantasy of somehow sharing a life with Ernie Watson, and she'd been doing it with no thought whatsoever of how her career was going to fit into that life. This new indifference about her work was nothing if not glaring; Nathan Williamson would never believe it.

She sighed heavily. "And Ernie thinks *I've* turned *his* life upside down," she said aloud. "Look at me. I'm sitting here waiting—talking to myself—when I *know* better. Just because he wants me to."

The key phrase was *he wants me to,* and she knew it. He'd helped her with Petey, probably kept her from losing the job she now felt indifferent about, and she knew she owed him that . . .

Who was she kidding? She was doing this because she was in love with the rascal; that was why she was doing it. She tossed her duffel bag into a corner before she stumbled over it again, and she set about the business of passing the time. She opened a can of tomato soup when she got hungry, and she found a small radio on the kitchen counter, which only picked up a local station, KTLQ. She read a paperback detective story she found in a magazine rack by the piano, and she tried not to think about Ernie and Elizabeth every time KTLQ played "You Still Move Me."

Desperate for something else to do, she decided to change her clothes. It was her policy to travel in comfort, so she'd only brought jeans, but she'd also packed one pale blue silk shirt. It was oversized, clingy, flagrantly sexy, and it gave her gray-green eyes more color. She'd brought it along for only one reason. She'd wanted him to see her in it, to see her womanliness enhanced as only soft, languid silk could do. She gave a mischievous smile as she put it on. She needed all the help she could get, and while a silk shirt was hardly the key to solving her problems, it certainly couldn't hurt.

But she grew more and more restless as the day stretched into early evening. It was getting dark, and her resolve was fading, silk or no silk. She was crazy to wait here, regardless of what Ernie wanted. She'd been foolish enough to tell him right out loud that she loved him, and she knew what kind of man he was. He'd want to tell her face to face that he was still involved with Elizabeth, and he'd want to make sure she was all right after he did it. He'd feel he had to buy her another Starlight hamburger and a brown milk shake to cheer her up, and then see her safely back to Dallas.

He'd make her feel better; he had a knack for it—with her, and with Elizabeth, and with Petey. She just didn't think she could stand it.

She put on her coat and grabbed up her duffel bag, hooking it over her shoulder and replacing the key on the nail on the porch rafter by the door. She looked back once at the dark house—when she passed the musical waterwheel. The evening was starry and cold and still except for *Swan Lake*, and she could hear the melody during almost the entire walk to Mim's.

There were no vehicles in Mim's yard, but she could see a light on in the kitchen. She walked up onto the porch and knocked loudly, but no one came to the door. She continued knocking for a moment, then sat down on the porch steps.

"This really hasn't been a good day," she muttered to herself. Something must be happening, she thought. Mim wouldn't tell her to walk over and then go off someplace. She sighed. There was nothing to do but walk back to Ernie's father's place. As desperate as she was to leave, the idea of thumbing her way along the highway didn't appeal to her at all. She waited a few minutes longer, until the cold drove her to start walking again. But cold or not, she lingered a moment at the

pond. She was always going to remember this place.
Always.

She was well into the yard before she noticed the
truck—Ernie's no-color pickup—parked close to the
porch the way her father had done. Her heart leaped.
She walked faster, looking at the empty truck and wondering why the lights on the house weren't on. She
crossed the porch, letting the screen door squeak and
slam, hesitating only a moment before she opened the
door and stepped inside.

"Ernie?" she called when she didn't immediately see
him. She was cold, and she swung her duffel bag to the
other shoulder so she could reach the switch near the
door. The lamps came on, and she stood blinking until
her eyes adjusted to the light.

Ernie looked at her gravely. He must have only just
come in, and he took off his hat and put it on the piano.
She couldn't tell what he was thinking and once again
she found herself having to wait.

"I . . . didn't think you'd be here," he said after what
seemed an eternity.

"I didn't think I'd be here, either," she answered
truthfully.

She stood rooted to the spot, loving him, despite the
hopelessness of their situation, loving his husky voice
and his sad eyes that searched hers, then went to the
duffel bag she was still carrying.

He took a few steps closer. "I guess you were leaving."

"Yes," she said quietly. She had lied to him before,
but she wasn't going to lie to him now. And, Lord, she
wanted to touch him. He looked so tired and so sad.

"Why?"

"Scared, I guess," she answered, still being truthful.

He smiled, the shy smile that always set her heart to pounding and turned her knees to mush. "Yeah, I've been pretty scared myself. You hungry?"

She made a gesture with her hand that was neither yes or no.

"Me either," he said, his voice going softer, huskier still. "You . . . going to come over here, then? I'd come over there, but my knee's killing me, and besides that, I don't know if you want me over there or not. I can't tell by looking at you—except that you're . . . not happy right now, and I don't know if I can do anything about that or not." He stopped talking when she dropped her duffel bag on the floor.

They stood staring at each other across the room.

"The hell with the knee," he decided, limping the distance between them. He stopped just short of touching her, his eyes traveling over her face. "You're so beautiful, you know that?"

"I've got freckles," she was quick to remind him, and he smiled again, making a gesture as if to touch her face, but not completing it, letting his hand fall to his side instead.

"Beautiful and special," he said, his eyes holding hers.

Oh, Lord, she thought. *This is where he tells me I'm a fine woman, but he's staying with Elizabeth.*

"Ernie—"

"Hannah, put your arms around me," he interrupted. "Will you do that?" His eyes still held hers, and she hesitated only a moment before she reached out for him, holding him tightly and pressing her face into his shirt so she could breathe in his heady masculine scent.

"Yes, I'll do that," she said, closing her eyes in relief because he hadn't said the words she'd expected and savoring his long sigh. Oh, he smelled so good to her, felt so good. They had a thousand things to talk about, to settle, and she didn't care about any of them. He was here, and that was all that mattered to her.

"I'm so glad to see you," he whispered. "I thought I'd messed up everything."

"Ernie, we have to talk," she said in spite of what she was feeling.

"Not now, Hannah."

"Ernie, I want to know about Elizabeth."

She meant that, and he knew it. He leaned back so he could see her face. "I took her to Tulsa."

"Tulsa," Hannah repeated.

He stepped away from her, as if he could tell her better if they weren't touching. He stood in the middle of the room, in his familiar thumbs-hooked-in-jeans-pockets stance. But eye contact between them was just as unsettling, and he looked away. "To the City of Faith Medical Center. There's a doctor there—he rides the rodeo sometimes. I thought he could help her get herself together, and I talked her into going—pretty much over Jake's dead body."

"This doctor—can he help her?"

"He can if she'll stop flying off in ten different directions. She's going to lose Petey if she keeps going the way she's going. That's what caused all this uproar in the first place. O'Day wants his kid, and Libby left Petey with me and you so he couldn't find her, which was a dumb stunt, doing it the way she did. I think she realizes that finally. We went to see a lawyer, too. He told her if she doesn't make some effort to show she's trying to straighten up, O'Day will get custody of his daughter, and there won't be a damn thing Jake and all his money can do about it. Half of Oklahoma and two-thirds of Texas know she left Petey with me and not her daddy. God, I'm tired," he said abruptly, sighing heavily. He looked up to meet her eyes. "I've told her how things are with me—about you."

She didn't say anything, and he went on.

"I love you, Hannah. I love you with all my heart, and I hurt you. I—it was the hardest thing I've ever done in my life, leaving you here when you didn't understand. The bad part is I can't say I wouldn't do it again if I had to. I'm not in love with Libby. I don't think I ever was, really. If I was in love with anything, it was what I *wanted* her to be, some idea of her I had in my mind that never really existed. My history with her is part of what I am—the same way my past with the bottle is part of what I am. And I want you to stay with me in spite of both of them. I know it's a lot to ask, Hannah."

He looked so miserable that she wanted to put her arms around him again, wanted to hold him tightly and never let go. But she stayed where she was.

"It's like what my old man told me about being alone. I didn't know I was lonely until the night I brought Petey to you. I need you, Hannah. Don't leave me."

The golden chance. It was all she'd wanted, all she'd dared hope for, and here it was after all.

I am afraid, Elizabeth! Maybe there is something wrong with both of us!

"Hannah, don't look at me like that," he warned her. "Don't. I love you. Don't look at me like that!"

Like Bambi, she supposed, tears welling up in her eyes. She hadn't meant to cry, but her mouth was quivering anyway.

"Ernie, we don't know each other. Not really. There hasn't been enough time for this."

"Tell me about it," he said, giving a resigned sigh. "You want to know what I think? I think some things you can't measure in time. I keep remembering something Mac McDade told me about his wife, Amelia. He was in a V.A. Hospital in New York City when he met her. He'd been wounded really bad in Southeast Asia, and she was married to somebody else. He said he was lying on a gurney out in the hall, and she came walking toward him. She had long black hair, and she was wearing a yellow summer dress. The sun was behind her all the way up that long hall, but he knew. Even before he saw her face, he knew she was the one. He waited ten years for her, and all that time he loved her without her knowing it. I think that's how it is with you and me, Hannah. Ten seconds from now, or ten years, I'm going to love you with all my heart just the way I do right this minute."

A hot tear slid down her cheek. "Ernie, I— Are you sure?"

"Am I sure?" he repeated incredulously. "Hannah Rose, would I act as crazy as I've been acting if I wasn't? It's the only thing I *am* sure about. Ah, Hannah, don't *cry*. I don't want you to be sad."

"This isn't sad," she said, her voice breaking. "This is like—the national anthem."

He threw back his head and laughed, that delighted chuckle she adored so, and he reached for her, hugging her to him hard. "Hannah, Hannah," he whispered against her ear, finally holding her at arm's length and smiling into her eyes.

But the smile faded, and his eyes grew dark and intense. She could see the passion there—and more. Uncertainty. He still had his own doubts and fears. He'd been hurt too badly not to be uncertain, but he was willing not to let their golden chance pass them by.

"Ernie?" she said, her eyes locked with his. "Could I . . . kiss you?"

There was the smile again, just as she'd hoped, quiet and shy and infinitely pleased. He didn't move. He waited, eyes open while she reached up with both hands to hold his face as she touched her mouth to his.

Lord, she loved the taste of him. He was sweetly, deliciously—Ernie. She kissed him to savor, enjoy, to arouse, and his eyes closed as he gave himself up to whatever else she wanted to do. She loved the soft feel of his mustache and the scratchy stubble of his beard.

"I love doing this," she murmured when she finally broke away. Her heart was pounding and her knees had gone weak.

"I'm kind of partial to it myself, Hannah Rose," he assured her, his voice strained and his breathing shaky. They both laughed, foreheads pressed together.

"Don't stop," he whispered.

She didn't, kissing him again and following one kiss with another until his lips parted and she could savor him even more deeply, until he could no longer be just the recipient, and he returned her attention with a knee-weakening kiss of his own.

"You're not going anywhere tonight, are you?" he asked, holding her tightly, keeping her head on his shoulder.

"No," she said contentedly.

"Am *I* going anywhere tonight?" he wondered, and she laughed softly, giving him a squeeze. He leaned back to look at her. "Am I?" he asked again, his dark eyes probing hers.

"No," she said again, and he grinned.

"You're sure?" he persisted.

"I'm sure." She reached up to touch his face, serious now. "You look so tired."

"I am. I didn't get much sleep." He covered her hand with his to keep it there for a moment, then kissed the the inside of her wrist. She felt it all the way to her toes.

He was staring into her eyes again, and she could see the weariness—and something else—just a touch of mischief. "Could we . . . go to bed?" he wondered further.

"Now?" she asked, as straight-faced as she could manage.

"Well, yeah. Now," he said nonchalantly. "Now is what I was thinking." He gave an innocent shrug.

She didn't answer, looking at him steadily, trying not to grin.

He raised both eyebrows, and she let go of a laugh. He hugged her to him, lifting her up off the floor, half carrying, half dragging her to the bed. He sat down, then flung himself backward, taking her along with him, so she was lying on top of him, her legs captured in his.

"There's something you ought to know, Miss Hannah," he whispered, his eyes full of devilment.

"What's that?" she whispered back.

"I'm not *that* tired."

She laughed, and he kissed her soundly to show her, then sat up, pulling her along with him. He took off her jacket and his, giving them both a sling toward the door. He looked down at the silk shirt she'd cunningly put on just for him, gently trailing his fingers over the swell of her breasts and making her nipples tighten and stand firm. Her eyes closed as he leaned down to gently kiss each one, his breath warm and exciting through the thin silk. She sat quietly while he undid the top button, then the next, and the next. His fingers trembled as he parted the shirt and unclasped the lacy wisp of a bra.

"So beautiful," he murmured as her breasts spilled forth. Once again he leaned down to kiss each one, making her head arch back and her hands slide into his hair as he began to suckle her. She gave a soft murmur of pleasure.

He moved away and began shedding his own clothes.

"Damn knee," he muttered once in the process of getting off his boots and jeans. She chuckled softly, holding her arms out to him when he was finally free of them, and he turned to her. She would have helped him with the rest of her clothes and his, but he caught her hands and gently put them aside.

"I've been lying awake nights thinking about undoing your buttons, Hannah. I want to do this."

But he didn't linger over it, finishing his task quickly, sliding under the covers with her, and fitting his body against hers. They were both cold, and they shivered against each other.

"I would have come after you," he whispered. "I would have come to Dallas. You know that, don't you?"

She pressed close to him, afraid she was going to cry again, and she told him the truth. "No."

"Hannah—"

"Ernie, hold me. Hold me . . ."

His arms tightened around her, and the tears slid out of the corners of her eyes. He began to kiss her then, slowly, deliberately. His breath warmed her skin as he pressed soft kisses, one by one over her shoulders and the swell of her breasts and back to her mouth again. "Don't cry, honey. It's going to be all right with us."

She shivered. "Is it?"

"Yes!" He buried his face in her neck. "I love you. I didn't want to hurt you, Hannah."

"Ernie, I know," she whispered. She did know that.

"I want you to understand. Tell me you understand."

"I understand," she whispered. "It just—wasn't easy."

"I was scared to death you'd be gone. I was scared I'd look into your eyes and I wouldn't see *me* there anymore."

She didn't tell him how close she'd come to going. She held him tightly instead. "Make love to me, Ernie. Now. I want you inside me; I need you."

"I need you, Hannah," he responded. He shifted her even closer so his mouth could take hers from every angle. His hands moved urgently over her bare back and the length of her body. Her breasts flattened against the hard planes of his chest.

"You feel so good to me," he told her. "I want to touch you. I want to taste you."

Her breasts were heavy, aching with desire, the nipples taut, and once again she moaned with pleasure as he touched and tasted. He reached down, lifting her leg over him so he could explore her more intimately.

"Oh," she whispered, writhing from the sheer pleasure of his hand sliding between her thighs, his fingers edging closer, touching her, not touching her, boldly yet gently parting, gently invading the very core of her desire for him. And she desired him. She was restless again, empty again. She wanted to be touched, filled as only he could fill her. She closed her eyes, giving in to his intimate probing. Her breathing grew more and more shallow, and her listless fingers trailed over his chest. She pressed a kiss against that patch of curling hair at his throat that had intrigued her so the night they met, her body suddenly arching at the exquisite sensations that stormed through her body. She clung to him desperately as the pleasure increased.

"Hannah—" he whispered, and she opened her eyes.

He was rolling onto his back, bringing her over him. His penetration was swift and deep and made them both moan. He held her tightly, and she rested her head on his shoulder for a moment, savoring all of it: the warm, clean smell of his skin, the rasp of his beard stubble against her face, the taste of his hungry kisses, the hot, aching feel of him inside her. But there was more to this than just a fitting together of bodies, so much more. He loved her and she belonged to him. Everything he did made her feel it. Perhaps there were things that couldn't be measured by time, she thought. She lifted her head to look into his eyes. Elizabeth wasn't here with them.

"I love you, Hannah Rose," he whispered, thrusting deep.

She wanted him deeper, and his breath caught, his fingers clutching at her hips as her response to the pleasure he gave her intensified his.

"I love you," she said, meaning it even more than the first time she'd said it.

"Tell me again."

"I love you, Ernie. Love you—!"

He was both gentle and fierce, and the surging tide of passion quickly overtook them. Soft murmurings of love gave way to impassioned cries of release, and then there was only the quiet, the gentle ebbing of a sweetness she would never forget.

She woke up because Ernie had cried out in his sleep. She called his name, but he cried out again.

She raised herself up on one elbow. "Ernie!" she said, shaking him hard.

"What? Wha—" he muttered, trying to wake up.

"You were having a bad dream. You were yelling in your sleep."

"I was . . . yelling?"

"Yes," she said worriedly. She wrapped her arms around him and held him close.

He chuckled in the darkness.

"Ernie?" she said, raising her head.

He chuckled again, pulling her around so they were lying spoon fashion, his arms and legs around her and his hands on her breasts. He kissed her on the neck and ear. And he laughed.

"Ernie—"

"I wasn't having a bad dream, Hannah Rose," he whispered, nibbling at her ear. "I dreamed I was making love with *you.*"

When she woke a second time, the sun was up and Ernie, already showered and dressed, was sitting on the side of the bed.

"Hannah, get up," he said. "We have to go."

"Go?" she said sleepily. She tried to burrow deeper under the Hudson Bay blanket, but he wouldn't let her.

"Hannah, come on. Honey—"

"Where are we going?"

"Back to Dallas. We'll stop by the ranch to see Libby before we go."

Hannah sat up, awake now. "I thought she was in Tulsa."

"No, she came back home. She'll be going to Tulsa twice a week. We're going to see her and Petey. And your daddy," he added.

She sat up, the blanket sliding off her bare shoulder. She covered up again, and she looked into Ernie's eyes. "I don't want to see Jake. We—had words."

Ernie grinned.

"He said *you* had the words."

"I thought you and Jake didn't get along," she said in exasperation. "Do you two tell each other *everything?*"

His grin broadened. He was so handsome this morning, freshly shaved, his mustache trimmed, his hair still damp and slicked down. "Well, not everything, Hannah Rose."

"You told him I didn't think he was my father," she accused him.

"Yeah, I did," he answered, clearly refusing to be put on the defensive. "That's what he wants to talk to you about."

"Ernie," she protested, but he kissed her on the nose and was up and heading for the door.

"I'll be back in a minute, Hannah. Put on your clothes, will you?" He looked around at her, turned away and sighed, then looked around at her again. "Well, maybe I'm not in *that* big a hurry," he decided, coming back to the bed. He tipped her backward without ceremony and threw a leg over her, making her laugh. "Don't hurt my knee," he warned her, a peculiar command, to her way of thinking, because he was definitely in the dominant position. His eyes were full of the devil again.

"How is your knee, by the way?" she asked just as his mouth was about to brush over hers.

"It hurts. Kiss me."

"Are you always this impetuous?" she asked, dodging his mouth again.

"Hannah, I don't even know what that means."

"It means—"

"Hannah!" he said in exasperation. "Do you want to get any kissing done here or not?"

"Yes, I want to get some kissing done here," she said. Among other things. She slid her arms around his neck and smiled into his eyes. Lord, she loved this man!

"Well, all right, then—oh, you better not look at me like that, Hannah Rose," he said, giving her another ominous-sounding warning.

"Why not?" she whispered, her mouth tentative, then insistent against his.

"Because—" he managed in the little breathing space she gave him.

"Because, why?" She reached down to pull his shirt-tail out, working until she could run her fingers over his bare back.

"Becau—"

She slid her tongue into his mouth to stop him from talking, and he gave a soft moan. She pulled the front of his shirt out as well, sticking her fingers as far inside his jeans as they could go.

He was laughing now, and she undid his belt and unsnapped his jeans. "Hannah, what are you doing!" She pulled the zipper down to give access to her inquisitive hands.

"Oh, *I* see what you're doing," he advised her.

"You did that on purpose," he accused her, his eyes closed, his clothes in disarray, their bodies still joined. He groaned. "Hannah, you are hell on a man with a bum knee." He tried to move, but only managed to groan again.

"I love you," she said by way of explanation, and he lifted his head to look deep into her eyes, kissing her mouth in a way that threatened to put his knee in jeopardy again.

"Hannah, Hannah," he whispered against her ear. "I thank God every day for it."

He suddenly laughed. "Woman, you didn't even let me get my clothes all the way off!"

"You didn't want your clothes all the way off," she reminded him.

"This is true," he admitted. He suddenly hugged her tightly, rotating his hips into hers. "God, I love you! Oh! You're going to have me on crutches!"

"Better me than some bull," she informed him, kissing him again and then helping him sit up.

"You're going to have to go see Jake," he said as he worked to disentangle his clothes.

"I know it." She looked up at him, giving him a funny lopsided smile, and he reached out to touch the side of her face.

"It's going to be okay," he told her.

She looked into his eyes. "He doesn't much like either one of us, Ernie."

"That's his loss, Hannah."

It was just the right thing to say, and she hugged him for a moment, then showered and dressed while he went on some errand in Tahlequah—breakfast, as it turned out—steak and eggs with biscuits and hot coffee and orange juice.

She was nervous about seeing her father—and Elizabeth for that matter—and she took a long time to get ready, fussing with her hair and makeup until Ernie finally intervened, putting his arms around her and holding her tightly and telling her the same thing he'd told her earlier. "It's going to be okay."

She looked up at him and forced a smile. "How bad can it be?" she decided.

"Damn right, Miss Hannah. Let's go."

She was looking forward to seeing Petey. She'd missed her chatter and her quiet but merry ways. She'd never seen the Browne ranch in person, just on occasional Christmas cards signed only by Elizabeth.

"Lord, it looks like—Southfork," she said as they turned into the broad paved driveway.

"Almost," Ernie agreed. He squeezed her hand once before they got out of the truck, then escorted her directly to the front door. He glanced at her as he rang the doorbell. "What?"

"Maybe I ought to use the service entrance."

"You're too uptown for that, Hannah Rose," he said, giving her a wink.

She smiled in return. It seemed to take a long while for the bell to stir up some activity in the house, but one of the great double doors finally opened.

"Mim!" Hannah said in surprise, gratefully accepting the hug Mim offered her. She had that familiar sense of recognition again—that Mim somehow smelled like her mother.

"See what a good idea it was to be strong and wait?" she whispered into Hannah's ear.

"I didn't expect to see you here," Hannah said.

"I didn't expect to *be* here," she said. "But thanks to John Ernest, our Elizabeth is going to live at home for now. And Petey. So it seems the Browne ranch needs a nursemaid again. Come in. Everyone's waiting."

This was precisely what Hannah dreaded. She glanced at Ernie as he followed Mim into the house, pressing her cheek into the hand he rested on her shoulder for a moment. The foyer was huge, with a slate floor and a chandelier. She wondered if the house had looked like this when her mother left it.

"Dear sweet Anna-Hannah!" she heard behind her, and Petey leaped at her almost before she could turn around.

"Dear sweet Petey!" Hannah cried in return, hugging her tightly. "I missed you!"

"I missed you, Anna-Hannah." They covered each other with real and fake kisses, laughing together at their mutual silliness.

"Hey," Ernie said, tapping Petey on the shoulder with one finger. "Remember me?"

"Dear sweet Ernie!" Petey said, growling at him the way he sometimes did when he was teasing.

"That's me." Ernie beamed at her, and she reached out to lock one arm around his neck, holding them together in the familiar three-way hug.

"I kiss *you* and I kiss *you*," she said, kissing them both on the cheek. "Want to see Rufus?"

"What's a Rufus?" Hannah asked. "Is he anything like a Cowpoke?"

"No, Anna-Hannah!" Petey cried.

"What is he, then?"

"He's a *cow!*" she said, wiggling to get down.

"He's a cow," Ernie advised Hannah, too. "Where's your mama, Pete?"

"I'm here," Elizabeth said from the doorway. Jake was with her. She looked tired, but much less so than the other night. And she was, as always, exquisitely beautiful. "If you'll all excuse us, I'd like to talk to Hannah alone."

She swept forward, locking her arm in Hannah's and leading her to a sun room off the foyer. It was a beautiful room with wicker and glass furniture, ceiling fans, and a forest of indoor plants. She let go of Hannah's arm, sitting down on a small sofa and patting the place beside her. "Ernie tells me congratulations are in order," she said as Hannah sat down.

"Elizabeth, don't." She looked into her sister's eyes until Elizabeth glanced away.

A gardener was trimming grass with a pair of hand clippers outside the tall glass windows, and Elizabeth stared in his direction.

"Daddy doesn't like for them to use mowers near the house when he's home," she said idly. "The noise gets on his nerves." She looked back at Hannah. "Are you in love with Ernie?"

"Yes," Hannah said quietly.

"It's a little—quick, isn't it? Not for me, of course; but then I've always been impulsive. But you, Hannah. You're supposed to be the one with her head on straight. You know a man two weeks, and you're in love with him?"

Hannah didn't answer.

"Well. Serves me right, I guess. I put the two of you together. I knew both of you would do about anything in the world I asked you to. Funny, though. I never even considered it—that you might . . . fall in love with each other."

She abruptly stood up. "I want you to be happy together, Hannah. I do. Don't let Daddy do anything that will ruin it for you. Don't get upset if he cuts you out of his will or something like that."

Hannah smiled. "I'm not in his will, Elizabeth."

"Yes, you are. Years and years ago. I saw it." She frowned. "Didn't I tell you?"

"No, Elizabeth."

"Oh, well," she said, shrugging. "Here comes Daddy

and Petey. I think I'd like to talk to Ernie now. You'll tell him I was . . . nice about things? The way he wanted?"

"I'll tell him."

"Come see Rufus, Anna-Hannah!" Petey cried, grabbing her hand.

"Hannah," Elizabeth said, pausing on her way out, "thank you for taking such good care of Petey."

"You're welcome," Hannah said.

Petey was pulling her toward an outside door. "Do you mind if I walk with you, Hannah?" Jake asked.

She looked at him gravely. This was his house, and she was in no position to mind or not.

"Petey, leave Hannah's arm hooked to her, will you? That way," he said, nodding toward the door that Petey was working so hard to get her to.

They walked out together, and Hannah caught a brief glimpse of Mim's worried face as the door closed behind them. The sun was bright, but the air was still chilly. She pulled her coat closer around her and walked at her father's side, thinking of all the times she'd imagined doing just this when she was a child. Petey danced on ahead, leading them across the drive and down a landscaped path toward a wooden fence.

"Hannah, wait," Jake said, catching her arm. "There's something I want to say to you—now, before I lose my nerve. I told you yesterday there wasn't a thing in this world I could do about being a father to you now, and there isn't. I'm not a man who makes apologies, but I want to tell you something about me and about your mama back then, so maybe you'll understand things better."

He stopped, glancing into her eyes, then looking away. "I'm a . . . proud man, Hannah. I'd appreciate it if you didn't repeat any of this to Watson." He looked back at her, but she didn't answer. She wasn't going to make any promises. Her mother was dead, and she was a grown woman. The past didn't matter now.

Jake Browne gave a long sigh. "You know, you remind me of myself, Hannah. You're not going to give me the time of day because you don't think I deserve it."

"That's the way you treat Ernie," she said quietly. He was about to say something, but apparently thought better of it.

"I'd best get on with it," he said instead. "I made up my mind to tell you this and I'm going to do it. I reckon I owe you that."

"You don't owe me anything—" Hannah began, but he held up his hand.

"When I was a young man, I fell head over heels in love with your mother. The only problem with that was she didn't love me. She liked me well enough, but she wasn't in love with me the way I was with her. I wasn't used to taking no for an answer. I was young. I was good-looking. And I had money and the arrogance to go with it. I courted your mother anyway. She was a strong woman, but she was no match for me when I had my mind made up. I kept after her until I wore her down. I *made* her say she'd marry me, just by sheer persistence, if nothing else. And she did it.

"She married me, but she wasn't happy with me. We had two babies, and she wanted to leave me—for no reason that I could see. I wasn't a bad husband—not great, maybe, but I never hit her or ran with other women or anything like that. I couldn't believe she wanted to go. My pride wouldn't let me believe it. I knew she never loved me, but I said there had to be some reason. She couldn't want to go off and leave a fine upstanding man like me for nothing. I said there was somebody else she wanted, somebody else she'd already had maybe. I convinced myself that you were this other man's child. I knew that wasn't so, but I said it anyway. I said it until I believed it—because my pride said I *had* to believe it.

"I think I must have been half crazy. I loved her, you see. I finally said she could go and be damned. She could take you, but she couldn't have *my* child. She tried every way she knew to talk me out of keeping Elizabeth. In the end she went with you. There were times when I'd have men on watch all night in case she came back and tried to steal Elizabeth. And she never gave up wanting her other baby until Elizabeth got old enough to be hurt by it."

Petey was calling, and he broke off, looking down the path. "She never forgave me for it. I guess I tried to make it up to Elizabeth for what I'd done to the two of you. You were right. I gave in to Elizabeth's every whim. Mim tried to tell me I was ruining her, but I couldn't say no to her. That's why she's like she is."

Hannah walked off from him a short way, her hands jammed into her pockets. *Such pain*, she thought. *Hers and Elizabeth's, her mother's, his. And for nothing. A man's pride*. She looked back at him.

"I had a good life," she said, wanting to hurt him and to comfort him all at the same time. To her surprise, he smiled.

"Oh, darlin', I know that. You lived with your mama. Your mama was a rare jewel. It couldn't have been otherwise."

He abruptly turned and walked away, leaving her with tears in her eyes and with Petey still calling her to come and see a cow named Rufus. She watched her father walk back toward the house, watched him meet and ignore Ernie along the way, only to whirl around and say something to him at the last minute.

Ernie listened to him, hooking his thumbs in his jeans pockets and staring straight ahead, and then walked on, apparently without comment.

"What did he say to you?" Hannah asked when he reached her. He took her hand and walked with her down the path toward the wooden fence where Petey stood petting Rufus.

"What did he say to *you?*" he countered, looking at her closely.

"I asked first."

Ernie grinned. "He said, Hannah Rose, that if I didn't treat you right, he'd kick my butt from here to Tucumcari—only with a little more colorful language."

She managed a smile, and he reached up to caress her cheek. "You okay?"

But she didn't have to answer. Petey was there, pulling her by the hand so she could marvel over someone's overgrown bovine 4-H project—a cow that seemed to think she was a dog. Hannah admired Rufus, joked with Petey and Ernie, laughed in all the right places, and when it was time to go, she even managed a few dry-eyed good-byes. Mim's was particularly difficult, because she clearly knew what Hannah's father had said to her, and she was kind enough not to comment. Hannah held Petey for a long time. But for her, she might never have met Ernie Watson. She hugged Elizabeth and gave Petey back to her. And that left only her father.

She stood for a moment, staring up at him. "Goodbye, Jake," she said finally, her voice low but steady. He gave a curt nod and walked away. He still wasn't a father to her, but he was a real person now. She knew what to call him at last. And he was right. Because of his revelation, she was beginning to understand. The only problem was that now she'd exchanged one pain for another. Such a waste, she kept thinking. Her father couldn't help being the kind of man he was, and her mother had lived out her life alone. How much had her traumatic marriage to Jake Browne had to do with that?

"I want to take you to New Mexico sometime," Ernie said a few minutes later, as they were riding over a back road toward Route 75. She was listening to him. It was just that she had burning eyes and a great lump in her throat she was going to have to do something about. "I've got some land around Chimayo. I want you to see it. I bought it when I was just a kid. See, when I get too slow to be a bull-dodging clown, what I want to do is live there and be a stockman for the rodeo. Anybody that's looked as many ornery critters in the eye as I have won't have any trouble picking them out to buy. I got some money put away. It shouldn't take too long to get a good string of rank bulls and horses—Are you okay?" he asked abruptly.

"I'm okay," she said, but she made the mistake of looking at him.

"Hannah, are you going to cry?"

"Yes, I think so," she answered, giving a long, wavering sigh.

"Then slide over here and let me put my arm around you while you do it."

She didn't hesitate, and he held her close to him, not asking her any questions, just letting her use him as a crying towel if that was what she needed. It wasn't for herself that she was crying; it was just that someone should mourn the agonizing demise of what might have been in her parents' lives, and she was the only one to do it.

She sat up, wiping her eyes with a red bandanna Ernie gave her.

He reached out to run his hand over her hair. "You want to talk about it?"

"No."

They rode for a time in silence, and he kept glancing at her.

"You want a Starlight Café hamburger?"

"No," she said.

"Neon sign," he reminded her.

"No," she said again, knowing what he was doing. But she didn't want to feel better just yet.

"I'm buying," he threw in as a further enticement.

"No."

"Ozelle might have her hair curlers out."

"No," she said, a smile working at the corner of her mouth. He was going to make her feel better in spite of herself.

"You want to get married?"

"N—what?"

"Do you want to get married?" he said distinctly. "To me," he added. "After I've courted you so you'll know I love you and I'm sure about it, and you'll know you love me and you're sure about it, and I'm back rodeoing and I've got some money coming in and—stuff like that."

For once in her life, television experience or not, she was totally speechless.

"Now, look, Hannah. You know I don't work up to

things. I love you. Well, what did you think?" he said a bit testily. "We were going to live in sin?"

"It—occurred to me."

He grinned. "It did?"

"Yes," she said, shameless to a fault.

"Damn!" he said, clearly pleased. "Except that won't work."

"It won't?" she said.

"No. When you come to Tahlequah with me at Christmastime, or when you go with me to New Mexico to see my godchildren or on the road buying rank bulls, or when you come to see me at the rodeo, I want to be able to say, 'This is my wife'—even if you've got one of those dang Perry Mason suits on."

"You do?" she said, staring straight ahead. This man was serious!

"And that's not even mentioning when we get pregnant."

She looked at him with such alarm that he suddenly pulled off the road by an abandoned roadside country store. The windows were boarded, and it was made of sagging, weathered wood and covered with rusty, illegible signs. The wind had picked up, and it buffeted the truck. Ernie reached for her, taking her into his arms and holding her close. She leaned into him, loving the feel of him, the way she always did.

"Hannah, whatever Jake said—it's not something that's going to hurt us, is it?"

She leaned back so she could see his eyes. "No. It's nothing to do with us."

He nodded, and he reached up to gently stroke her cheek with the backs of his fingers. He took her into his arms again, kissing her deeply, lovingly. "We're a pair, Hannah Rose," he said with a sigh.

She hugged him tightly and smiled, knowing the past was as abandoned as the old country store behind him. "You know what, Watson? I think maybe we are."

EPILOGUE

HANNAH CAME STRAIGHT from KHRB, arriving late and out of breath and just in time for the introduction. She hadn't stopped to change clothes, and she was still wearing high-heeled shoes and a Perry Mason suit—red, but Perry Mason nevertheless.

"Ladies and gentlemen," said the rodeo announcer, "welcome to Will Rogers Coliseum. While we're waiting for the next event, I'd like to introduce one of our professional rodeo clowns. You've seen him out here working tonight—protecting the cowboys in these events. A fine athlete and gentleman—Mr. John Ernest Watson! Take a bow, Ernie!"

The spotlights came on in the middle of the arena, and Hannah couldn't keep from grinning. She loved him in clown face—actually she loved him in any kind of face—but she especially loved his flagrantly corny rodeo routines. Ernie had on a big black hat and a black and white striped referee's shirt and cut-off baggy jeans with black tights and knee-high black and yellow rugby socks and orange Day-Glo suspenders. He had red and blue bandannas pinned up one corner all around his waist, and he was the most beautiful thing Hannah had ever seen. She moved closer to the front to get a better look, parting a group of cowboys who seemed unusually happy to see her.

"So, Ernie! Tell us how you've been doing!" the rodeo announcer said.

Ernie took his hat off and held it over his heart. "Not so good, Red!" He picked up one corner of a bandanna and carefully wiped his eyes.

"Why, Ernie, what's the matter, son?"

He blew his nose loudly, then announced: "My wife died!"

"She died! Ernie! We're sorry to hear that! What in the world happened to her!"

"Poison mushrooms!"

"Poison mushrooms! Ernie, that's awful! I'm really sorry!"

Ernie put his hat back on and let go of his bandanna. "Naw, that's all right, Red!"

"That's all right!"

"Yeah, that's all right. I got married again!"

"You got married again?"

"Yeah, I got married again!"

"So how's this wife doing?"

Ernie took his hat off again and held it over his heart, and Hannah couldn't keep from chuckling. "Aw, she died, too, Red!"

"She died, too! Well, what in the world happened?"

"Poison mushrooms!" Ernie declared.

"Poison mushrooms! You don't mean to tell me! Ernie, I am sorry!"

Ernie put his hat back on. "Naw, that's all right, Red! I got married again!"

"You got married again? Ernie—and I'm afraid to ask this, folks—how is this wife doing?"

Slowly, Ernie took his hat off again and placed it over his heart, standing for a long moment in the middle of the arena to give the crowd time to react. He wiped his eyes. He blew his nose. He wiped his eyes again. "She died, Red!"

"Ernie, no! What happened?"

"Strangulation!"

"*Strangulation!* Strangulation? How did that happen!"

"She wouldn't eat the mushrooms!" Ernie bellowed.

Hannah laughed and applauded with the rest of the crowd. She'd heard that routine a hundred times in the past few months, and she still loved it.

"John Ernest Watson, ladies and gentlemen! Now, before Ernie goes off someplace, I just want to say he really hasn't run through three wives. In fact, this old bachelor here just got married today! And we want to give him a big round of applause to show him we wish him the best!"

Ernie held up his hand to acknowledge the applause.

"This is one dedicated man, ladies and gentlemen. Just got married this afternoon and here he is working on his wedding night. When you leaving on your honeymoon, Ernie?"

"One hour, twenty-seven minutes, and thirteen seconds," he yelled, to the delight of the crowd, glancing in Hannah's direction, but likely seeing the big cowboy behind her who was jumping up and down and waving his hat.

"Red!" Ernie called to the announcer.

"Yeah, Ernie, what is it?"

"My wife had to work tonight, too."

"She had to work tonight too? Ernie, this is getting to be as bad as that other story you just told me. I'm sorry to hear that, son."

"Naw, that's all right, Red! She just got here!" he yelled back, and Hannah realized what the big cowboy was jumping up and down about.

"She just got here? She's here tonight? Your bride's here?"

"Yeah!"

"I hate to tell you this, son, but this ain't no place to spend your honeymoon. Well—where is she, Ernie?" he asked when the laughter had died down.

There was a drumroll. Spotlights were sweeping the audience, and Hannah would have made a run for it but for the wall of cowboys that blocked her exit.

"You're husband's looking for you, ma'am," one of them advised her with a grin, turning her around and pointing her toward the wall that separated the audience from the arena. Down close, she could barely see over it, but Ernie wasn't letting a minor detail like that bother him. He was up and over the wall with the same agility he would have used to elude a vindictive bull.

He walked up to her slowly, in a blaze of spotlights, pausing dramatically until Hannah was ready to bolt again—standing in front of a television camera was nothing compared to this! His eyes were full of mischief and he slowly, slowly reached inside his shirt to present her with . . . a single red rose.

She was in his arms then, smearing his greasepaint, and the cheering around them was deafening.

"You're not going to cry, are you?" he asked the woman who couldn't make it through the national anthem.

"Yes!" she said, holding on to him for dear life.

"Ladies and gentlemen," the announcer shouted, "I give you Mr. and Mrs. John Ernest Watson!"

"I love you with all my heart," Ernie whispered into her ear, and she smiled. She loved him with all her heart, too. She had loved him almost from the very beginning. Her smile widened, and she looked around at the crowd of still applauding people.

When John Ernest Watson said he wanted to tell the world: "That's my wife," he *meant* it.

Second Chance At Love

COMING NEXT MONTH

ANGEL ON MY SHOULDER #428
by Jackie Leigh

Angel Faye Darnell has fled fame and
fortune as a glitzy country singer to live
quietly incognito in the Rockies. But
sexy mountain man Gus Cougar changes
her plans, making Angel's new life more
dramatic—and passionate—than ever!

RULES OF THE HEART #429
by Samantha Quinn

Natasha O'Reilly is a fiery, funny
Bohemian, and William St. James is a
wealthy, proper entrepreneur. But these
opposites attract like fire to kindling,
and when Natasha moves into his house
to renovate it, their reservations are
stripped away with the wallpaper...

Second Chance At Love

Be Sure to Read These New Releases!

ALL THAT JAZZ #424
by Carole Buck
Jazz O'Leary doubts her blood's blue
enough for Ethan Wilding, but he takes her
troubled teenage protégés in stride and
reformed bad-girl Jazz into his arms
and heart, clearing her of complicity
in a computer scam, and even
decking an FBI agent!

IT STARTED WITH A KISS #425
by Kit Windham
Bridesmaid Henrietta Jones jumps out
of a bachelor-party cake into the arms of
best man Sam Marchand. Impulsively,
Sam gives her a grandstand kiss...
and the rest is chemistry!
Sam's con-man grandfather and Henrietta's
coterie of male admirers add humor.

Order on opposite page